THE FLICKERING TORCH MYSTERY

TWO unexplainable plane crashes near an airport on the East Coast plunge Frank and Joe Hardy into a bizarre case.

When their famous detective father is called to New York City by a group of insurance companies to investigate air freight thefts at Kennedy International Airport, Mr. Hardy asks Frank and Joe to take over his current case of the suspicious plane accidents.

From the moment Frank and Joe find a radioactive engine in an airplane junkyard, unexpected dangers strike like lightning. Despite the repeated attempts on their lives, the teen-age detectives pursue their investigation and make a second startling discovery involving contraband uranium isotopes. These two vital clues and others that Frank and Joe unearth provide the solution to one of the most baffling mysteries the boys and Mr. Hardy have ever encountered.

*The force of the man's blow caused Joe
to lose his balance!*

Hardy Boys Mystery Stories

THE FLICKERING TORCH MYSTERY

BY

FRANKLIN W. DIXON

NEW YORK
GROSSET & DUNLAP
A NATIONAL GENERAL COMPANY
Publishers

CONTENTS

CHAPTER I

Mysterious Accidents

"Boys, I'm on a new case and I've run into a problem," Fenton Hardy said. He had walked into his sons' second-floor bedroom, which was vibrating from the sounds of Joe's guitar.

"Sorry, Dad," said the seventeen-year-old blond boy. "Didn't hear you come in. Frank and I were testing this new amplifier." He set down the guitar as Mr. Hardy took a seat.

"What's the matter?" asked Frank, dark-haired and a year older than his brother. "Can we help in any way?"

"I think so," his father replied. "This case has me up a tree. It's a baffling mystery. In fact, two of them. A couple of light planes crashed recently near Marlin Crag Airport outside Beemerville. They were coming in from the sea for a landing and hit the cliffs. Both pilots died."

1

"What a shame," Frank said. Both he and Joe were licensed pilots and shared the comradery of fliers.

"Any theories?" Joe asked.

"Weather conditions were bad in both cases. Heavy fog. But the two men, Jack Scott and Martin Weiss, were experienced and could have come in on instruments."

"I take it the Federal Aviation Agency has investigated?" Frank said.

"Right. Now Scott's family has asked me to look into it. Sam Radley's done some preliminary work."

Fenton Hardy was world-renowned as a sleuth. Trained in the New York City Police Department, he had resigned to become a private investigator in Bayport, a medium-sized town on the East Coast.

His sons were following in his footsteps. Starting with the mystery of *The Tower Treasure*, Frank and Joe had proved their detective ability. Most recently they had cracked a tough case, *The Clue of the Broken Blade*.

Sam Radley was Fenton Hardy's assistant. A skillful operative, he could be relied on to stick to a case till it was solved.

"Sam obtained taped interviews with the Scott family," Mr. Hardy continued. "I'd like you boys to listen to them when he returns to Bayport in a few days."

"Meanwhile our assignment is to snoop around Marlin Crag Airport," Frank concluded.

"Exactly. Ask questions. Talk to the manager and find out if anyone knows any details about the crashes. You can fly up in our plane."

"It would be easier to go by car," Joe said.

"I know. But with the plane you can take the same approach as those pilots did and perhaps learn something as to why they crashed."

Mr. Hardy showed his sons a piece of paper with the flight route of the two planes.

"Now all we need to start out are the aircraft and engine numbers," Frank said.

"I've got them right here," Mr. Hardy said and handed him another piece of paper. The numbers were neatly typed in two columns.

"What about you, Dad?" Frank inquired. "Will we see you in Beemerville?"

"No. I'll be in New York working on a case for some insurance companies. They're worried about a ring of freight thieves who have been hitting the airports. Millions of dollars are involved."

"So we'll be on our own," Joe commented.

Fenton Hardy nodded. "Play it by ear, and I'll get in touch with you as soon as I can."

He rose from the chair and slapped Frank on the shoulder. "Continue your guitar practice. You both can drive me to the airport in a couple of hours and start your case tomorrow."

As their father went down the stairs, Frank said, "Okay, let's try the amp again."

Joe started playing a folk rock number. The amplifier picked up the sound and sent it reverberating through the house.

Frank and Joe were getting ready for a rock festival at the local park. They had a combo, in which Joe played the lead guitar. Frank handled the rhythm guitar. Three of their friends were on the other instruments—Biff Hooper bass guitar, Phil Cohen at the portable organ, and Tony Prito on the drums.

Moments later, above the sound of the twanging strings, the boys heard the rackety cough of a backfiring motor. A battered jalopy bucked along and jolted to a stop in front of the Hardy house. A plump youth with a freckled face eased out from behind the wheel.

Joe went to the window and chuckled. "Chet's music doesn't turn me on, Frank. I wish he'd trade the ancient heap in for a later model—like 1950, perhaps."

The Hardys ran downstairs and met their friend on the porch. Chet Morton, who lived on a farm outside of Bayport, was bubbling with excitement.

"What's up?" Frank inquired.

"Up is right! Up in the air! I'm building me a flying machine!"

Frank and Joe knew all about Chet's mania

"Okay, let's try the amp again!" Frank said

for hobbies. Almost every time they saw their chum he was involved in a new project.

"It'll take a jumbo jet to lift you off the ground," Joe needled their hefty visitor.

"Aw, cut it out," Chet protested. "I'm serious. Look. You know Beemerville?"

The Hardys exchanged glances. "Sure, it's sixty miles up the coast from here," Frank replied. "What about it?"

"It has an airplane junkyard. Mountains of old motors, fuselages, wheels—everything. Just the place for me to collect the parts for my plane. But I need your help."

"Why?" Frank queried.

"Well, you guys are licensed pilots, right? You even fly your father's plane. I want you to come along and help me pick out what I need."

"We've got a few weeks before the rock festival," Joe mused and gave his brother a knowing wink.

Frank clapped Chet on the shoulder. "All right, we'll go with you."

"You will? Terrific!"

"See you at the airport tomorrow morning at eight," Frank said.

"You want to fly? But it's only a little over an hour by car!"

"Well, we're combining the trip with a little assignment for Dad," Joe said and explained their mission to Chet.

"Oh, I see. I'm only second fiddle," Chet said with a grin. "Well, I don't mind. See you tomorrow!"

The next day was Saturday. Chet was waiting when the Hardys arrived at the airport. Frank, at the controls of their single-engine aircraft, took off smoothly and the shoreline flashed past beneath their wings. The sixty miles passed quickly. When they came in sight of Marlin Crag Airport, Frank swung out to sea in a big arc.

Then he turned back inland again toward the airport about two miles ahead. "This is the approach Scott and Weiss took," he said to Joe.

"Boy, these cliffs are for real!" Chet exclaimed. "They're like an accordion, the way the rocks wave in and out."

"And that oil refinery to the right looks like a beacon," Joe said. "You can't miss the high pipe burning off gas."

Glancing down, they saw the surf breaking over a rugged headland studded with huge boulders. The high escarpment fell in a sheer drop to the rocks below.

"Frank, watch it," Joe cried suddenly.

A light plane zoomed up under their left wing. They could see the face of the pilot, a square-jawed fellow with a long scar along his left cheek. Frank veered to the right to let the other pilot swish past under his left wing with little room to spare!

"Some nerve that guy's got!" Chet exploded.

"He just wasn't paying any attention," said Frank. Wiping some beads of perspiration from his face, he added, "At least I hope it was just negligence and he didn't do it on purpose!"

"He's going into Marlin Crag," Joe observed. "Maybe we can have a little talk with him when we land."

"I'll talk to him all right!" Chet said, flexing his muscles. "I'll show him— Hey, there's the airplane junkyard!"

Excitedly he pointed below to a large enclosed area with piles of plane parts strewn about.

"Okay, Chet, we'll check it out as soon as we're finished at the airport," Frank promised and radioed the tower for permission to land.

Soon they were in the office of Airport Manager Steve Holmes, a short, slender man with a high forehead. He identified the reckless pilot as Dale Nettleton. "But he's left already," Holmes added, "so I'm afraid you won't be able to speak to him."

"Too bad," Frank said, then changed the subject. "Mr. Holmes, can you give us any information on the Scott and Weiss crashes?"

"Both flights originated in Morrisville, New Jersey. The reason for the accidents must have been bad weather conditions."

"Where are the wrecks now?"

"I have no idea."

A man came into the room and was introduced

as Bill Zinn, the assistant manager. Of average build, he walked with a rolling gait, and his manner was breezy.

"Why are you interested in those two accidents?" he asked with a quick smile.

"We might be using this airport in the future," Frank said casually. "So we'd like to know if there's any danger."

"Like hitting the cliffs," Joe said.

"No danger at all," Zinn said affably. "Not if you know how to fly." He turned and left the office seconds before a teen-age youth entered.

"Hi, Hal," Holmes greeted him. "We were just speaking about the crashes." He turned to his visitors. "Boys, this is Hal McGuirk. He's an airport buff and hangs around here all the time."

"What do you know about the accidents?" Joe asked Hal.

"Really nothing. Except about a week before he crashed, I saw Scott spin down out of an overcast. He pulled up in time, but I wondered what caused it."

Holmes looked surprised. "Did you tell the FAA investigators?"

Hal shook his head. "Nobody asked me."

Frank said, "That definitely sounds like instrument trouble."

"Well, fellows," Chet pleaded, "let's get on to the airplane junkyard."

"Okay, flyboy," Joe said.

"Have you got enough energy to walk over there? It's at least a couple of miles," Frank teased their chubby friend.

"Oh," Hal said, "you flew in. I can drive you in my car, if you want."

"Hey, that's great. Thanks a lot!" Chet grinned.

As the Hardys were saying good-by to the airport manager, Chet, impatient to get to the junkyard, opened the door and strode out. He nearly collided wth Zinn, who mumbled something and hurried off.

When Frank, Joe, and Hal came out of the office, Chet whispered to the Hardys, "That guy Zinn was eavesdropping on us!"

CHAPTER II

Engine Trouble

FRANK and Joe were dumbfounded. As they walked through the lobby, they saw Zinn enter a telephone booth at the other end of the long hall.

"I wonder what he's up to," Frank mumbled to Joe.

They stopped for a quick sandwich, then continued on to the junkyard. It was located on gently sloping land surrounded by a sheet-metal fence. The place was crammed with fuselages, wings, engines and other parts from planes that had either been wrecked or retired because of old age. In one corner stood a boxlike structure, obviously the office. A giant crane was moving parts from one spot to another.

"Boy, this place is cool!" Chet exulted.

"The owner's name is O. K. Mudd," Hal said. "Here he comes now."

Approaching was a thick-set man in work

clothes with a bullethead and bushy black brows. His slit eyes took in the visitors with quick movements. Then he flashed a wide smile.

"What can I do for you?" he asked.

When Chet expressed an interest in buying airplane parts, Mudd invited them to look around while he went over to talk to the crane operator.

As Chet examined some fuselages, Joe poked through a pile of small engines. Suddenly Joe straightened up and gestured to Frank.

"Know what this is?" he asked, running a finger across the number of an engine.

Frank gasped. "Scott's engine. What do you—?" He broke off when he saw Mudd approaching.

"Have you found anything that interests you?" he asked. "This engine here's no good, but if you want to look over there, you'll see a few in pretty decent shape."

He pointed to a corner of the enclosure, where a mound of parts was covered with a heavy tarpaulin. As Frank and Joe walked toward the heap, Chet suddenly screamed, "Watch out!"

The giant crane had swung up over their heads with an airplane wing. The jaws opened, and the wing came hurtling down at the Hardys!

Frank threw himself to one side in a judo roll. Joe lunged in the opposite direction, but slipped in a patch of oil and hit the ground face down. Instinctively he clasped his arms over his head for protection.

The heavy plane wing smashed between the Hardys, sending up a cloud of dust.

Frank got up. "Are you all right, Joe?" he called out.

Chet and Frank pulled Joe shakily to his feet. He flexed the fingers of his left hand before replying, "I got a pretty good bang on the arm from the wing tip, but I'll live."

They looked around. The crane had stopped. The operator was scowling at them from his cab and Mudd rushed over. "What do you guys mean getting in the way?" he stormed. "You might have been killed!"

The boys were flabbergasted. Joe exclaimed, "It wasn't our fault!" He pointed to the crane. "It was that stupid—"

The junkyard proprietor flushed angrily. "Don't give me any of your lip, wise guy! Now beat it!"

Frank was suspicious of Mudd's unreasonable behavior, but decided that further argument would be futile.

"Let's go," he muttered to his companions.

Hal, who had watched the whole thing in a state of frozen shock, led the way back to the car. "I don't know what got into old Mudd," he said. "He's usually a pretty agreeable guy. He should have apologized instead of yelling at you. If I were you, I'd sue him for negligence!"

"He might have been afraid of just that," Frank

said, "and therefore wanted to shift the blame on us. By the way, what time is it? My watch stopped."

"Four-thirty," Joe replied.

"Five o'clock," Chet said.

"That's funny," Joe observed. "Mine stopped too!"

"And at the same time as mine," Frank stated.

"Maybe it was the shock when you hit the ground," Hal suggested.

"Possible. We'll have to take them to the watchmaker Monday."

The Hardys thanked Hal. "We'll be back here soon," Joe said. "See you then."

"I won't be around for a while," the boy replied. "Going to California to visit my aunt for two weeks."

Joe grinned. "Lucky you. Have fun!"

Early Monday morning the Hardys took their electric watches to the jeweler. He examined their interior mechanisms and whistled in disbelief.

"The quartz crystal oscillators have been damaged," he said. "Have you been fooling around with any radioactive material?"

"Not that we know of," Frank replied.

"Maybe there was some in that junkyard," Joe said.

The watchmaker was curious. "What junkyard has fissionable material? That could be quite dangerous."

Frank evaded the question and said, "Can you fix the watches?"

"Yes. But it will take a couple of weeks."

He took their names and address promising to send a postcard when the timepieces were ready.

As the Hardys drove home, Joe mulled over the jeweler's theory concerning the cause of the trouble with their watches. "We didn't get much chance to case Mudd's place," he said. "He could have an atom smasher hidden somewhere for all we know."

"There's something fishy up in Beemerville," Frank agreed. "We'd better have another look-see."

Sam Radley was waiting for them in the house. Fenton Hardy's assistant drew a cassette from his pocket. "I recorded this at Jack Scott's home," he said. "I got interviews with his wife, son, and daughter. What they said doesn't solve the mystery of Jack's crash, as far as I can tell. Well, you boys might spot something I missed."

The three adjourned to the Hardys' lab, where Joe placed the cassette in the machine and pressed the "on" button. They could hear Sam asking questions, and the members of Scott's family answering as best they could.

The first side of the tape told about Scott's background. His wife and children insisted he was an honest, hard-working man who enjoyed being a pilot. They stressed his clean flying record, which showed no accidents until his fatal crack-up against the cliff at Marlin Crag.

The tape petered out. Joe turned it over. Mrs. Scott's voice came through. She told about her husband's job.

"Jack flew a taxi service from Morrisville to Marlin Crag."

"Mrs. Scott, did Jack always carry passengers?" Sam asked.

"No, sometimes he made deliveries."

"What kind?"

"I don't know, Mr. Radley."

"Do you have any clues at all?"

"There's only one thing I can think of. Several weeks before his accident Jack received a call. He took it in the hall while the rest of us were in the dining room. He carried on a long conversation, and sounded excited and angry."

"What did he say?"

"Something about a flickering torch."

"Did you hear any explanation?"

"No. Jack put the phone down, came over, and closed the door. We couldn't hear any more."

"Did he mention the subject when he returned to the dining room?"

"No. He seemed upset, though. Obviously didn't want to talk about it. So I didn't ask."

"Was that like Jack?"

"No, not at all. That's why I remember the incident."

The tape went dead. "That's it," Sam declared, snapping off the machine. "What do you make of it?"

"The flickering torch might be the vital clue we need," Frank said.

"Sure," Joe added. "Maybe Jack Scott meant a beacon. He might have referred to that oil refinery near Marlin Crag Airport!"

"The high pipe burning gas!" Frank exclaimed. "It's a flickering torch if I ever saw one."

"Maybe the flame from the pipe lured Scott off course," Joe said.

Sam agreed. "That's a possibility."

"But how can we explain Scott's spin out of the overcast at the airport before his accident?" Frank asked. "Oh, I forgot you haven't heard about that, Sam." Quickly he clued Radley in about Hal McGuirk's observation.

"That's odd," Sam commented. "An experienced pilot isn't supposed to go into a sudden spin like that."

"Maybe his gyro horizon conked out," Joe said. "That would mean big trouble."

The three probed the problem for a while without finding any solution. Sam promised to investigate the oil refinery before he left, and the boys decided to go ahead with their plan to revisit Mudd's airplane junkyard in Beemerville. They phoned Chet, who agreed to come along.

They got out their Geiger counter, a metal box

about as large as a medium-sized dictionary. They made sure it was in working order and stowed it in the trunk of their convertible.

Then they donned special coveralls under their clothes to protect themselves against possible radiation.

"I'll take one for Chet, too, just in case," Frank said.

Chet Morton was waiting when they arrived at his house. He quickly put on the coverall, then they set out for Beemerville.

"The car makes more sense than the plane on this trip," Frank said as he kept the convertible wheeling steadily along.

"Better for a quick getaway, too," Joe noted.

Chet glanced suspiciously at his two pals. "Listen, you guys, if this is a getaway car, don't get away without me!"

Joe grinned. "What's the matter? Getting cold feet?"

Chet pretended to be hurt. "When did I ever get cold feet?" he asked plaintively.

"This is your last chance to quit," Frank said as he brought the car to a stop in a vacant alley behind the airplane junkyard. "We're headed for enemy country."

He took the Geiger counter out of the trunk and led the way to the back gate.

"The place seems deserted," Joe said. "Not even a watchman on duty."

"Maybe Mudd's in the office," Frank said and tried the gate handle. "Unlocked. Come on." He pushed the barrier open and slipped through, closely followed by his companions.

They looked cautiously around. The crane was parked near the office. Frank gestured toward the pile where Joe had discovered the engine to Jack Scott's plane.

"That's our objective," he said. "Let's not waste any time. No telling when we'll have Mudd's hired hands breathing down our necks. Chet, you and Joe stand guard. I'll make the test as fast as I can."

Joe and Chet moved off while Frank advanced to the engines. Reading the numbers, he finally spotted the one from Scott's plane.

Gingerly he shifted the Geiger counter close to the engine. The box began to emit a clicking sound. Frank glanced knowingly at Joe and Chet, who were positioned some distance away.

Scott's engine was radioactive!

Suddenly the office door slammed loudly. Footsteps could be heard coming around the building at a rapid pace.

Joe signaled to Frank, who ran toward Chet and tossed the Geiger counter to him. "Quick," he whispered, "stash this in the car."

As Chet darted back to the gate, Mudd came around the corner and strode up to Frank and Joe. Had he spotted the Geiger counter?

CHAPTER III

Frank Springs a Trap

"Just a minute!" O. K. Mudd called out. "I want to talk to you!"

He walked with his jaw thrust out and his fists clenched. Coming to a halt a couple of feet away, he broke into a friendly smile.

"I didn't want you to get away before I had a chance to show you some new things," Mudd declared. "A shipment of airplane parts came in early this morning."

The Hardys were surprised by the man's change of demeanor.

"Oh, I know what you think," Mudd continued. "The other day I wasn't exactly a bosom buddy of yours. Got up on the wrong side of the bed, I expect. It just wasn't my day. No hard feelings, I hope."

"Forget it, Mr. Mudd," Frank replied. "We weren't bothered by what happened."

"But your brother got hurt when the airplane wing fell. How's the arm, young man?" he asked, turning to Joe.

"Bruised, but otherwise ready for a fast game of tennis," Joe assured him.

"That accident wasn't your fault," Mudd said. "The crane operator shouldn't have let the wing drop. Now, back to business. Do you see anything you'd like to buy?"

"There's one item we're interested in," Joe answered. He pointed to Scott's engine.

Mudd smiled again. Rubbing the palms of his hands together, he responded, "But of course. If that's what you want, that's what you'll have. How much were you thinking of paying for this model?"

Frank promptly mentioned a ridiculously low figure.

Mudd hesitated and frowned. He looked down at the engine and then at Frank, finally flashing his smile again.

"It's yours. I admit it's battered, so I'll let it go at a sacrifice. How will you cart it away?"

"We have our car outside," Joe said.

"I doubt that it will fit," Mudd objected.

"Well, let's try it anyhow." Joe went to get the convertible and rode back with Chet.

By now Frank was holding his checkbook in one hand and a pen in the other, ready to pay for their purchase.

Frank had barely written the date on the check when the boys heard a thundering rattle of heavy wheels. Startled, they turned around in time to see a junkyard truck bearing down on them. Nobody was at the wheel!

The boys leaped aside and the truck smashed into their convertible with a sickening *crunch!*

Frank groaned. "It just had a new paint job!"

"Good night! What rotten luck!" Mudd declared.

Chet walked around the two vehicles, examining them with a practiced eye. "Your car isn't ruined, Frank," he said. "But it'll sure need some repair work!"

"So will my truck," Mudd declared. "However, I'll see that they're both fixed. My driver parked without setting the hand brake, so I'll be glad to pay up. I admit it's my responsibility."

"We'll be without a car for a while," Joe said glumly.

Frank shrugged. "Can't be helped."

"No sense in getting uptight about it," Chet declared.

"Nice of you to take the accident so calmly," Mudd commented. He summoned a tow car and had the convertible taken to a repair shop in Beemerville. The three boys rode along.

"This job'll take a week," said the mechanic.

"Okay, we'll leave it," Frank told him. He

opened the trunk and removed the Geiger counter, then gave the key to the mechanic.

The boys left and strolled down Beemerville's Main Street.

"What'll we do now?" Chet asked.

"Well, we still own the engine in the junkyard," Joe observed. "And we don't want to lose track of it after all our trouble. We've got to find out why it's radioactive."

"Let's take it now!" Frank urged. "I noticed a trucking firm down the street. We can have a pickup truck haul the engine to Bayport."

"Sure thing," the trucker said when they explained the assignment to him. "I haul lots of airplane parts from the junkyard. In fact, Mr. Mudd just called me about a job. It'll tie me up for an hour or so. But I can make the run down to Bayport later this afternoon."

"Fair enough," Frank said. "We'll meet you at the junkyard in an hour. We haven't had lunch yet, anyway."

Chet beamed. "Lunch! Follow me, men!"

Joe grinned. "Meaning you've spotted a likely place to stow away some grub." The Hardys knew there was nothing Chet liked better than eating.

"I'm with you," Frank said. "My inner man craves sustenance, too. Where shall we go?"

"An eatery down the block," Chet said. "I noticed it while we were riding the tow truck."

The three walked to the diner, settled into a booth, and ordered.

"Say, this chow is great!" Chet exclaimed after sampling the food on his plate. "I picked the right place!"

"Must be the best diner in Beemerville," Joe agreed.

Frank, however, was deep in thought and hardly noticed what he was eating. "There's something going on at that junkyard," he said gravely. "Every time we show up there we have an accident. I'm sure Mudd is the cause. But why?"

"It's strange, all right," Joe agreed. "What's his game?"

"Well, now that I feel better," said Chet, patting his belt buckle, "I'm ready for any of O. K.'s tricks."

"All right," Frank said with a grin, draining his glass. "Let's go back and load up the engine."

"Don't forget," Chet reminded him, "I'm here to buy a fuselage. So far you guys have had all the action."

"Well, select what you want and the truck can take it, too," Joe said.

They left the diner and strolled back to the junkyard. Suddenly Frank stopped, grabbed Joe by the elbow, and pointed to the pile of engines.

Scott's engine was gone!

"Maybe Mudd had it moved," Joe said.

"We'll soon find out," Frank answered. "I saw

him in his office when we walked by the window. Let's ask him what gives."

Mudd greeted them with an apologetic smile. "Too bad about that engine, boys," he said. "Another customer came in about an hour ago. He bought it."

"But you agreed to sell it to us!" Joe reminded him.

"Sure. You were ready to take our check," Frank protested.

Mudd smirked. "I never took your check, however. So it was no deal."

Frank shrugged helplessly.

"You see," the junkyard owner went on in an oily tone, "this customer made a much better offer than you did. And paid cash."

Joe winced.

"Don't worry," Mudd went on. "I have lots of other engines, better ones, too."

"All right," Frank muttered. "We'll look around."

"And I want a fuselage," Chet said.

The boys left the office.

"Joe, while Chet's checking out fuselages, let's see if we can't find the engine from Martin Weiss's plane," Frank suggested.

The Hardys split up and met again half an hour later. Neither had spotted anything.

"What do you make of this whole thing?" Joe asked his brother.

"Well, this much is pretty obvious," Frank said. "Mudd removed the engine because he didn't want us to have it. In order to delay us, he had our car wrecked."

Joe nodded. "Questions: Did he know it was Jack Scott's engine? Did he know it was radioactive? Did he see our Geiger counter and realize we knew it, too?"

"I wish we had the answers," Frank replied. "Maybe we'll find them if we find the engine."

Just then Chet returned, bursting with enthusiasm. "I got me a fuselage. Made a deal with Mr. Mudd. I'll pay him in installments. Makes it easier on the Chet Morton pocketbook."

Their hired pickup swung through the gate and the boys explained that the cargo for Bayport would be a fuselage instead of an engine.

The crane lifted Chet's purchase into the back of the truck, where Chet decided to ride. Frank and Joe sat in the cab.

The driver took it slow and easy at first, edging around corners and through traffic until he made the turn onto the highway. Then he shifted into high.

Nothing was said for a while. Frank, acting on a hunch, broke the silence.

"Was the job Mudd had for you this morning a tough one?" he asked.

The driver gave him a shifty-eyed glance. "Oh, not too bad."

"No big cargo to move?"

"Well, it wasn't a jet plane," the driver joked without further explanation.

Noting his evasiveness, Frank decided to spring a trap on him. The Hardys' detective training had taught them that an unexpected question often did the trick with a suspect.

"Wasn't it funny about that engine?" Frank asked suddenly, looking hard at the driver.

The man became tense, his hands gripping the wheel. He caught his breath and stared down the highway as if hypnotized.

"Why would anyone want to do that with an old piece of junk?" Frank pressed the point home, watching the man intently.

The driver relaxed. "Oh, so you know about it? O. K. told me the job was a secret. All very hush-hush. He didn't let on you guys were in on the operation."

Frank laughed loudly. So did Joe, who was backing Frank up.

"We've been in on it from the beginning," Frank said. "Only O. K. didn't tell us in advance about shifting the engine today."

The driver snickered. "Since you guys know so much, maybe *you* can tell me why Mudd had me drop the thing over the Marlin Crag Cliffs!"

CHAPTER IV

Boat Crash

THE Hardys were thunderstruck by the driver's story. For a few seconds there was silence.

Finally Frank remarked casually, "I guess Mr. Mudd didn't have any use for that engine."

"It was kind of beaten up," Joe added. "We couldn't care less what happened to it."

"Me neither," the driver said.

After they had driven a little more than an hour, the trucker said, "Bayport's just ahead. Where do you want me to go?"

"The Morton Farm," Frank replied. "It's on the edge of town. Take the road to the right."

After bumping for a couple of miles over a roughly tarred surface, they came to a mailbox marked "Morton." The driver turned into the entranceway and braked to a halt beside the house.

Gleefully Chet jumped out of the back. He supervised while the other three lifted the fuselage off. "Right here, under this shed," he called out. "Easy now, I don't want it damaged."

"Your pal likes giving orders, don't he?" the driver grumbled. "Why don't he give us a hand?"

"He figures his brain is the most important part of the operation," Frank puffed.

"You guys are hurting my feelings," Chet said, finally grasping the fuselage. "Anybody'd think I was lazy."

Frank and Joe laughed as they released their burden and allowed it to settle into place under the shed. Chet paid the trucker, who stepped up into the cab and set off for Beemerville.

Then Chet drove his friends to their home.

"Well, I'm glad to see you're in time for dinner!" a familiar voice greeted them.

The speaker was their Aunt Gertrude. Although extremely fond of her two nephews, she never missed an opportunity to chide them about the dangerous risks they took when working on an assignment.

"We made a special effort to be on time, Aunty," Frank said soothingly.

"We wouldn't stand up the best cook in Bayport," Joe chimed in.

"You're a couple of flatterers," Miss Hardy said, laughing. She looked pleased just the same. "Your mother and I are just about to serve. Hurry up!"

Mrs. Hardy, a slim, pretty woman, greeted her sons with a hug as they sat down at the table.

After the meal Frank and Joe went to their room and discussed O. K. Mudd and his suspicious actions.

"We know the radioactive engine was dumped over the cliffs," Frank began, "but we don't know where. That means we'll have to search along the shore."

Joe nodded. "We can do it in the *Sleuth*."

The *Sleuth* was their powerboat. They kept it in a boathouse on Barmet Bay near their home, and used it mostly for fun. But several times the Hardys had relied on their craft in searching for criminals along the coast.

"What about the tides?" Joe asked.

Frank went to a cabinet where they stored their maritime charts. He removed one containing information about the tides of Marlin Crag, and placed it flat on the table.

"It's a pretty narrow shore," Joe commented, leaning over his shoulder.

Frank agreed. "That means we'll have to wait for low tide. The engine might have tipped out away from the cliffs. Could be under water at high tide."

Next morning, after a hearty breakfast of pancakes, sausage and eggs, Frank and Joe drove to the boathouse and eased the *Sleuth* out into the open water. It was a sleek craft powered by a rugged inboard motor.

Frank took the wheel. The propeller churned

the water into a white froth and the powerboat roared across the bay.

"Let's see what she can do!" Joe yelled into the wind.

Frank gave it full throttle and curved around in a big circle in the middle of the bay. He drove the *Sleuth* toward shore, zipped between two small islands, followed the buoys and veered back out again. He slowed the craft suddenly, went into reverse, and then raced straight forward again at top speed. Finally he cut the power and allowed the boat to idle.

"That was a good warming up," Joe said. He added, "Look, what's that coming?"

A dot in the distance began to grow larger on the surface of the bay. Another powerboat was headed in their direction.

"Hey, it's Tony Prito's *Napoli!*" Frank exclaimed.

Tony was a dark-haired, lively youth whose father ran a construction company in Bayport.

"Who's that with him?" Joe inquired.

Frank shaded his eyes with his hand. "Biff Hooper is my guess. He's too big to be anybody else."

Biff was a husky six-footer who knew how to use his fists when the going got rough. He and Tony had been in on several of the Hardys' investigations, and many a criminal had felt the iron of Biff's wallop.

The *Napoli* pulled alongside the *Sleuth* and they bobbed up and down together in the waves.

"Hi, you guys," Tony saluted the Hardys. "What are you doing?"

"Trawling for flounder?" Biff quipped. "Or have you got some crooks on the line?" He reached a big hand out to grasp the *Sleuth*'s gunwale and held the boats together.

"We've got a nibble, I'd say," Frank replied and explained the situation.

"So you see," he concluded, "we've got to scout the shore below the Marlin Crag Cliffs."

"Can we help?" Biff asked.

"That's an idea! How about making this a combined operation? Joe and I will scout the shore. You and Tony could drive along the top of the cliffs. That way we can look for clues in both places."

"Sure," Tony agreed. "We may find the spot where the truck stopped. That'll be where the engine went over."

"Then you flag us," Joe suggested, "and we'll know just where to look."

Suddenly the *Sleuth*'s ship-to-shore radio began to squawk. Frank answered. "Why, Aunt Gertrude," he said in surprise, "what's the matter?"

"It's about Chet Morton," she declared in a worried voice.

"What about Chet?"

"His airplane fuselage has been stolen!"

"What? How did that happen?" asked Joe, who had been listening in.

"Chet wasn't there at the time. His mother saw a big truck with two men drive into the yard. She thought Chet had hired them, and didn't pay much attention."

"And the men loaded up the fuselage and left?" Frank asked in a perplexed voice.

"Right. Anyway, Chet's waiting for you at the farm."

"We'll get there as fast as we can," Frank promised.

He told their friends what had happened and they postponed their trip to the next day. Then Frank and Joe pushed away from the *Napoli* and the *Sleuth* churned toward the shore. Frank's mind was on the fuselage. He said, "Joe, do you think—?"

"Look out!" Joe shouted. "A floating log!"

Too late! The bow of the powerboat struck the log and careened over it. Frank and Joe flew head over heels into the bay.

Frank went down until his lungs began to pound. Kicking violently, he shot back to the surface and looked for Joe, who bobbed up beside him, puffing and spluttering. They swam to their boat and clung to its sides until the *Napoli* raced up to them.

"Lucky we saw what happened," Tony called out.

"Any chance of getting to shore under your own power?" Biff inquired.

The Hardys clambered on board and examined the engine. "No go," Joe reported.

"All right. We'll give you a tow," Biff said, tossing a rope aboard.

Frank and Joe felt discouraged when they reached shore. "We'll never be able to use the *Sleuth* tomorrow for our investigation," Frank lamented.

"No problem. Take the *Napoli*," Tony offered.

"Thanks, that's great," Frank said gratefully. "It'll change our plan, though. You'll handle your own boat. Suppose Joe goes with you. Biff and I will scout the cliffs by car."

Frank's idea was accepted unanimously. The disabled *Sleuth* was berthed for repair and the *Napoli* purred off. Frank and Joe jumped into their car and headed for the Morton farm.

There they met Callie Shaw and Chet's sister Iola in the driveway.

Vivacious and carefree, blond Callie was Frank's favorite date. Iola, who had dark hair and dimples, usually paired off with Joe. It turned out that the girls had arrived just in time to see the truck leaving.

"What company did it belong to?" Frank asked.

Callie's brown eyes searched for an answer. "I couldn't tell," she said. "There was no name on it."

"Did you get the license number?" Joe said.

"Sorry," Iola replied. "That was covered with mud."

Further questions revealed that the girls did not get a look at the men in the cab, neither had Mrs. Morton.

At that moment Chet stormed out of the shed where he had been looking for clues. "This is outrageous robbery!" he fumed.

"An airplane engine and a fuselage disappear without apparent reason," Frank observed. "Could there be a connection between them?"

"Find one, maybe we find both," Joe suggested.

"If we could locate the truck it would help," Frank said. "What did it look like?"

The girls gave a description as best they could.

"Well, it wasn't the one we hired to bring the fuselage down here," Frank said.

"What's at the bottom of all this?" Chet groaned.

Joe looked grim. "That's what we'll have to find out, Chet!"

"Meanwhile," Iola put in, "don't forget you've got some practicing to do here tonight!"

Joe slapped his forehead. "Our combo! Is this the night?"

"Sure is," Callie answered. "And the rest of us expect you to be here."

"We will," Frank promised. Then the Hardys left.

Phil Cohen was the first to arrive at the Morton barn that evening. A thoughtful, handsome youth, and a good student, he usually had a book in his pocket. Phil was another of the Hardys' dependable allies when it came to solving cases.

As the others entered, Phil played a few chords on the organ which was kept in the barn where the boys usually practiced. "The grand entrance!" he boomed. "A fanfare for the world's greatest detectives!"

Frank grinned. "It's good to know that we're appreciated around here."

"You Hardys got it all wrong," Biff quipped. "Phil was referring to Tony and me!"

Everyone laughed. Then Frank called the group to order. He adjusted the new amplifier, and they swung into a piece of country music. But the rhythmic sound could not cheer up Chet, who sat by gloomily, thinking about his prized fuselage.

The young musicians practiced for an hour and a half before piling into the kitchen for cokes and sandwiches.

"Come on, Chet, buck up," Joe said. "That fuselage would be pretty hard to hide. The police will find it!"

"Yeah, at the bottom of a cliff, maybe!" Chet muttered.

In the morning Frank and Joe stopped at headquarters to see Chief Collig. He was a husky man with a weathered face, who had often co-operated with Fenton Hardy on his cases and was fond of Frank and Joe.

Collig held out a broad hand as the boys entered. "I guess you're here about the theft at Chet's place," he said. "That was a pretty bold heist all right."

Frank nodded. "Any leads, Chief?"

"Not a one so far. But we're working on it!"

After their talk with the chief, Frank and Joe proceeded to the dock where they met Biff and Tony. Frank and Biff climbed into Biff's father's station wagon.

"We'll do some sleuthing while we're waiting for you up there," Frank said.

"Okay, good luck!" Joe waved to them as he boarded the *Napoli* with Tony. He stowed the Geiger counter, also some food they had brought in case they decided to stay overnight. Then they started up the coast. After a few hours they ran into heavy fog.

"Bad visibility," Tony said, frowning.

"Better slow down," Joe cautioned. "Somebody might be—"

Joe never had a chance to finish his warning. A big fishing boat loomed up out of the fog, ca-reening along at full speed. In a second the larger craft would smash into the *Napoli!*

CHAPTER V

Fire in the Night

IN desperation, Tony spun the wheel sharply to the right. The nose of the *Napoli* swung beneath the tall bow of the fishing boat. Its stern swerved past with a grinding noise as the two craft bumped.

The powerboat bounced off, bucking and pitching in waves created by the bigger vessel. The two boys were drenched in a deluge of spray that broke over them.

Joe wiped salt water out of his eyes. "Quick thinking, Tony," he gasped. "I thought we'd had it!"

"We didn't miss it by much," Tony muttered. "Anyway, the fog is lifting. I can see the cliffs at Marlin Crag."

They scouted the shoreline beneath the cliffs for an hour without sighting anything.

"Well, suppose we try the cove next," Tony

said. He guided the boat carefully between the rocks studding the surf. Reaching the shore safely, he and Joe dragged the bow of the *Napoli* up on the sand.

They walked along the beach for a mile or so, peering behind boulders and scuffing sand piles with their feet.

"Nothing here," Joe said finally.

Then a voice called down to them from the top of the cliff. Looking up, they saw Frank and Biff.

Frank cupped his hands to his mouth and shouted, "We may be on to something. Tire tracks leading to the edge of the cliff!"

"A car or small truck has been here," Biff called down. "This could be the spot where the engine was thrown over. It might have landed where you guys are standing."

Joe looked at the incoming tide. "We'll check it out later," he said. "The water's getting too high to do anything now."

"The boat!" Tony exclaimed. "She'll hit the rocks if we don't get her out of the cove!"

He and Joe raced down the beach. The *Napoli* was bobbing in heavy breakers when they got there. Her hull banged ominously against a jagged outcropping of rock.

Frantically they pushed the powerboat away from the shore. Tony started the motor. He sped through the entrance of the cove and into calmer waters.

"Boy, the *Napoli* had another close call that time!" he exclaimed. "This isn't our day!"

They discussed their situation over sandwiches as darkness sifted down over Marlin Crag. The gloom was pierced by a licking flame high in the air. Subsiding for a moment, it blazed up again, tossing wildly in a rising wind.

"Good night! What's that?" Tony said.

"An oil refinery. It's a high pipe burning off the excess gas. Frank and I noticed it when we flew up here."

The pipe itself was no longer visible, but the flames flickered eerily in the growing darkness as if they were disembodied spirits in the sky.

"Sure looks spooky, Joe."

"What we were wondering," Joe said, "is whether that's the flickering torch Jack Scott referred to. It might have pulled him off course."

"Deliberately, you mean?"

Joe nodded soberly. "Someone could have turned the flame up as Scott was coming in for a landing. He might have thought it was a beacon at the Marlin Crag Airport."

"I get it," Tony said. "Scott would have flown into the cliff without knowing it."

As he spoke, a roaring sound overhead caused the boys to glance up. A plane zoomed through the darkness toward the airport.

"I hope that fellow makes a better landing than

Jack Scott," Joe muttered. "He seems to be wobbling. Or is he?"

The pilot dipped his left wing. Spiraling down, he made a wide circle, straightened out, and headed right for the *Napoli*.

"He's buzzing us!" Tony yelled. "Hit the deck!" The boys ducked. Joe turned his head to get a look at the plane.

It zipped over them with only yards to spare. The roar of the engine nearly deafened them. The backwash of air rocked their boat violently.

For a split second the pilot glared down at them. Then he gained altitude and disappeared over the cliffs in the direction of the airport.

Tony picked himself up. "Friend of yours?" he asked.

"It looked like Nettleton's plane, Tony. But I couldn't tell whether that was he flying or not. We'd better contact Frank and Biff."

Taking out a code blinker, Joe flashed signals to the top of the cliff. When Frank answered, Joe proposed a get-together at a deserted wharf nearby. "Will do," Frank signaled back.

After tying up the *Napoli*, the four held a conference at the wharf.

"The guy who buzzed us might be back," Biff said. "He knows we're here."

"And he might bring a gang with him," Frank warned.

"So we'd better stick together," Tony suggested.

"Let's take our sleeping bags and find a protected spot over there where those shrubs are," Joe said, pointing, "instead of sleeping in the boat."

"Good idea," Frank agreed. "And we'll take turns standing guard so we don't get taken by surprise. Suppose Tony takes the first watch, Biff the second, Joe the third, and me the last, okay?"

They found a good hiding place not far from the wharf and soon everyone but Tony was sound asleep. When his watch was over, he woke Biff, who did his turn and was succeeded by Joe.

The younger Hardy settled himself for his stint. Suddenly, in the stillness of the night, he heard a board creak. Rising to a crouching position, he peered through the darkness.

Dimly he could see someone slipping stealthily across the wharf toward the powerboat. The stranger carried a steel bar in his hand.

Joe had no time to wake the others. He raced forward on tiptoe, and jumped the intruder from behind. They went down in a tangle of arms and legs. The steel bar clattered onto the wharf.

Joe and his adversary rolled over and over. For a moment they teetered at the water's edge. Joe felt the man's hand under his chin, forcing his head back. Desperately he broke the hold. They wrestled wildly back over the boards.

By now the others were wide awake. Seeing Joe

They went down in a tangle of arms and legs

locked in combat with the intruder, they scrambled to their feet and came charging forward. But the stranger managed to break away from Joe. Jumping up, he dashed across the wharf and vanished.

The boys took up the chase, but finally had to give up and returned to the wharf.

"We lost him!" Biff complained disgustedly.

"At least he didn't have a chance to sabotage the *Napoli*," Frank remarked. "Did you get a good look at him, Joe?"

"No. It was too dark."

Frank stooped and picked up the steel bar. "Imagine what that guy could have done to Tony's boat with this!"

Tony shuddered. "I don't know about you," he said, "but I won't get any more shut-eye now!"

"Well, it's almost daylight," Frank noted. "Since I didn't have to stand watch, I'll go for coffee and buns."

He trudged to an all-night diner on the road to the airport. Half an hour later Frank was back. The boys eagerly munched the rolls and drank the coffee.

Afterward, Biff gathered the cups and waxed paper, put the debris in the bag, and deposited it in a litter basket on the wharf. He and Frank then returned to the top of the cliff, while Joe and Tony boarded the *Napoli* for a run back to the beach.

The tide was out. Tony jumped out into the wet sand. Joe followed with the Geiger counter. After a search of about twenty minutes, Tony suddenly ran toward a couple of rocks at the water's edge.

"Joe, here it is!" he called out excitedly.

An airplane engine was wedged in the sand between the rocks. Joe scraped the number clean.

"Scott's engine, all right," he said. "Let's get it out."

"How about taking a reading on the Geiger counter first to make sure it isn't dangerous?" Tony suggested.

"Okay." Joe ran the instrument over the battered metal and the needle showed a small amount of radioactivity. "That's not enough to be harmful," he remarked.

They dug the sand away. Hauling and straining, they rolled the engine up the beach toward the cliff. Here Joe took another test.

"The vacuum pump shows the highest reading," he said.

"Why's that?"

"Search me. Let's take a closer look."

They examined the vacuum pump housing at the rear of the engine. The vacuum line was broken off, allowing a view of the interior.

"That's funny," Joe exclaimed, "the housing's empty! The works have been taken out. Now why would an experienced pilot like Jack Scott be flying without a vacuum pump? He should have known that without it he would lose control of the plane when flying on instruments in bad weather."

"Maybe it fell out during the crash," Tony theorized.

"Could be," Joe admitted. "But why is the housing radioactive? That's the real puzzler. Anyway, we might find some answers when we put the engine through the lab test."

"How are we going to get it home, by boat or car?" Tony asked.

"I think it'd be easier by car," Joe said. "It might be rather heavy on the boat, especially if we hit rough water."

He called up the cliff to Frank and Biff, announced the discovery of the engine, and told them to drop a rope.

Biff did so, attaching the other end of the rope to the bumper of the station wagon.

The boys below wrapped the rope around the engine, fastened it securely, then signaled to Biff. He started the car. The rope tightened, lifting the burden clear off the ground. Foot by foot it rose toward the top of the bluff.

Halfway up, however, the rope frayed, then snapped! The heavy airplane engine plummeted!

CHAPTER VI

The Stolen Fuselage

JOE and Tony scrambled for safety as the engine hurtled down. It struck a jutting rock, ricocheted off, and flipped over the boys' heads into deep water.

Chips of stone and a heavy shower of powdered rock enveloped the two boys. Coughing and sneezing, they stumbled away and collapsed onto the sand. There they lay gasping for breath.

"I nearly choked," Joe said when he was able to speak.

"Me too," Tony wheezed, wiping dust from his eyes. "Boy, that engine didn't miss us by much!"

"You guys all right?" Frank called anxiously.

"We will be, soon as we can breathe again," Tony replied.

"What about the engine?" came Biff's voice.

"It's underwater. We'll need a stronger rope."

"Don't have one."

"Then we'll have to leave it until later," Joe said.

Frank agreed. "We might as well make tracks for Bayport. Let's have a powwow at our house."

He and Biff got into the car and drove off. Joe and Tony took the *Napoli* out into deep water for the run down the coast.

Later in the day they all gathered at the Hardy home. Frank phoned Chet to come over. Mrs. Hardy served refreshments in the living room.

Frank and Tony occupied the sofa. Joe and Biff took the easy chairs. Chet sprawled on the floor, propping himself on one elbow. He had a tall glass of milk and a big plateful of crackers within easy reach.

"How about giving out with some info," Chet said, downing a long gulp.

The others described their adventures at Marlin Crag.

Chet whistled softly under his breath. "Wow! You're lucky to be in one piece!"

Biff nibbled on a cracker. "Somebody's out to change that. But who? Mudd? If so, why?"

"Whoever it is has a good spy system," Tony said. "They knew we found Scott's engine!"

Joe nodded. "That's why that roughneck tried to stave in our boat. They thought we were taking the engine out by sea!"

Frank considered the whole problem. "Since it's too late to take the *Napoli* back to Marlin

Crag today, our best bet now is to start a search for Chet's missing fuselage."

Chet swallowed the remains of a cracker and reached for another. "I'm with you on that, Frank!"

Frank chuckled. "I knew you'd be. Anyway, the fuselage is pretty big. The gang would have trouble hiding it."

"They hid it from the police quite successfully," Chet muttered.

Biff and Tony had to go home, so it was decided that the Hardys and Chet would scour the area between Bayport and Marlin Crag by car.

Frank wanted to check with the police first and called headquarters. He asked the sergeant on the desk whether any sign of the fuselage had been reported.

"You'll have to talk louder," said the sergeant. "This is a bad connection. I can hardly hear you."

Frank repeated his question.

"Oh, yes," came the reply. "Take the highway north past the bridge, turn right, and continue a mile. You'll find it right there."

"What luck!" Frank exclaimed as he hung up. "Let's go!"

He, Joe, and Chet hurried out of the house and piled into the Hardys' family car. Frank headed north at speed limit.

Spotting the bridge, he turned right. "Must be a dump we're looking for. Keep your eyes open.

I'll clock the speedometer at exactly one mile, as the sergeant said."

Frank slowed down when they covered that distance. "See anything?" he asked.

"Nothing," Joe reported.

They continued on until they saw a motel ahead.

"Might as well turn around there," Frank decided. "We must have missed it." He drew up in the motel driveway. The words on a large bright neon sign glared: HUGHIE'S LODGE.

The truth hit the trio at the same time. Despite their disappointment, they burst out laughing.

"Frank," Joe chortled, "when you said fuselage the sergeant must have mistaken it for Hughie's Lodge!"

After discussing their predicament, the boys decided to look at the big dumps northward from Bayport to Marlin Crag. At the first three they drew a blank.

"This plan isn't working," Joe said, discouraged.

Chet sniffed. "Looking is better than doing nothing, Joe!"

"Let's try one more," Frank proposed. "If we score another goose egg, maybe we'll come up with a new plan."

The next dump was approximately halfway between Bayport and Marlin Crag. Frank drove in and circled past mountains of debris, some of it smoking from spontaneous combustion.

They were nearly at the exit when Chet called out, "Hold it, Frank. I see something!"

As the car stopped, Chet scrambled out in great excitement. He ran behind a pile of broken furniture and other discarded household items. A moment later he exclaimed, "I've found it!"

Frank and Joe ran over to see the lost fuselage, which looked none the worse than when Chet had bought it. All three began to drag the cumbersome load out onto level ground.

The Hardys examined what had once been the cockpit of the airplane. "Here's the number," Frank said. "Looks pretty well smudged, but I can make it out. Chet should make a note of it."

He called off the number, one figure at a time. Suddenly he stood up straight. "Joe! You know whose plane this is from?"

"The one Martin Weiss was flying when he cracked into the Marlin Crag cliff!" Joe said in a strained voice.

Frank circled around the rear, where he paused for a longer inspection. "Something bothers me," he said.

"What's that, Frank?" Chet asked.

"The tailpost and the rear wheel are missing!"

"So?"

"It was there when you bought the thing."

"Well, maybe it fell off in transport. What's a tailpost, anyway?" Chet asked.

"A hollow metal tube," Frank explained. "It controls the movements of the rear wheel."

"First we find Scott's engine, with a missing vacuum pump, then Weiss's fuselage with a missing tailpost," Joe mused. "And Mudd doesn't want us to have either."

"We have no proof that Mudd stole the fuselage," Frank objected.

"No proof, but I don't have any doubt."

"I'm with you," Frank said. "Well, let's get this thing back to the farm, okay?"

The boys hired a local trucker to cart the fuselage to Bayport. Chet could hardly wait for his bulky prize to be unloaded.

Joe winked. "Suppose you fly us to Marlin Crag next time. We could use a crack pilot."

"Sorry, Joe," Chet replied. "I'm off your case. This baby will take up all my time." He patted the fuselage affectionately.

"You'd better lock it up," Frank suggested, "so it won't disappear again."

He and Joe helped Chet move the fuselage into the barn, then they left. At home they found Sam Radley, who had just come from the oil refinery at Marlin Crag.

"The Gamble Oil Company, which operates the refinery," he reported, "is a reputable firm. They burn off their excess gas at odd times, and

I've been told that no one can manipulate the flame. Also, the pilots know about the stack and its location and could hardly be lured off course by it."

Frank was disappointed. "Not much to go on," he said glumly.

"No. And I drew another blank," Sam went on. "Tried to get hold of Martin Weiss's parents, but they weren't home. Neighbors tell me they'll be back tomorrow. Suppose you fellows ride down to Pittston and interview them?"

"Glad to," Frank said.

"What about the radioactive engine?" Joe queried.

"We'll pick that up on the way home. Let's take a block and tackle this time."

"And Biff. We'll need his muscle. I'll call him," Joe said.

Eager to get on with the case, the boys left early the next morning and drove to the Weiss home, a modest cottage in the center of Pittston. The pilot's parents received them cordially, and after explaining their mission, Frank plunged directly into questioning.

"Mr. Weiss," he began, "do the words 'flickering torch' mean anything to you?"

The man nodded. "Yes. Martin went there many times!"

CHAPTER VII

Down the Cliff

FRANK and Joe were elated to find the answer to the riddle.

"What is the Flickering Torch?" Frank asked eagerly.

"It's a restaurant, not far from Beemerville," Mr. Weiss told them.

Frank and Joe stared at each other.

"Why did Martin go to the Flickering Torch?" Frank asked.

"Well, my son liked country music. A combo plays there weekends," Mr. Weiss explained. "Also, he met his friends there. The place was popular with the crowd from the airport."

"Did Martin ever tell you the names of his buddies?" Joe said.

Their host shook his head.

"But that was all over anyway," Mrs. Weiss

spoke up. "About a week before the crash Martin said he didn't like the Flickering Torch any more. Besides, he was quitting his job!"

"Why would he do that, Mrs. Weiss?" Frank inquired.

"He didn't like flying the taxi service between Morrisville and Marlin Crag. Something about it was getting on his nerves."

"We don't know what was bothering him," Mr. Weiss continued. "Do you think it had anything to do with his accident?"

"We intend to find out," Frank said.

"Well, I do hope we've been of some assistance," Mrs. Weiss murmured as she and her husband showed the boys to the door.

"You've both been very helpful," Frank assured her. "Now that you've identified the Flickering Torch for us, we can check it out."

"We might find the clue to the mystery there," Joe added.

As Frank, Joe, and Biff left Pittston, the sky grew ominously dark, and by the time they were halfway to Marlin Crag, a heavy rainstorm broke loose. It swept in from the sea in blinding sheets.

"Oh, great!" Biff groaned. "How are we going to get the engine in this kind of weather?"

"The waves will be pounding against the cliffs," Frank said. He flipped on the car radio for the weather forecast.

The announcer said, "Rain through early afternoon, tapering off by this evening. Drive carefully."

"Well, that's that," Joe declared. "Let's go home, have lunch, and wait till it clears up."

On the way back to Bayport the boys discussed the latest break in the case.

"We're going to hear some real cool folk rock pretty soon," said Frank, skillfully maneuvering in and out of the traffic.

"At the Flickering Torch, you mean?" Biff asked.

"Right. We can take the girls, too. Mix dancing with detective work."

They dropped Biff off at his house, then went home. Shortly after they had arrived, the phone rang. Joe answered, then gestured to Frank to listen in.

The caller was Fenton Hardy, who asked for a briefing on the Marlin Crag case.

Frank and Joe took turns describing the events of the past few days. "Dad, what do you think is our best lead now?" Frank ended the recital.

"The radioactive engine," Mr. Hardy replied. "The low yield reported by the Geiger counter may not be too significant. But it could be the debris of a large amount of some radioactive substance."

The detective pointed out that strict laws governed the handling of subatomic energy. "The hot stuff is too dangerous to be left lying around,"

Mr. Hardy said. "People who handle it illegally often do just that. Some of them couldn't care less who gets a lethal dose of radiation."

"Do you believe that Scott transported radioactive material illegally?" Frank asked.

"Who knows? We'll have to find out more about it."

Joe said that he and Frank intended to go back to Marlin Crag for the engine as soon as the rain had let up. "We'll put it through a lab test," he declared. "Maybe we can isolate the radioactive element."

After they had discussed all possible angles to the mystery, Frank asked about his father's investigation.

"I'm making some progress by posing as a hood," Mr. Hardy revealed. "I've discovered the stolen goods from the airport are being hauled away in trucks. Destination unknown. That's where you fellows come in."

"How?" his sons asked in unison.

"While hobnobbing with the crooks I located an informer who's willing to talk—for a price. Trouble is, he won't say anything to me or Sam Radley. He's afraid we'd be spotted and the mob might give him a one-way trip to the bottom of the bay."

"And you mean Joe and I can contact him without causing suspicion?" Frank asked.

"Exactly."

"Where do we find him?" Joe asked.

"I can't tell you yet. He's to let me know in a few days. When he does, I'll get back to you. Be ready to move quickly. And remember, this is a dangerous mission. You may run into some tough customers. Keep your wits about you."

"Okay, Dad."

After Mr. Hardy had hung up, Frank and Joe decided to hold another conference with their friends. Joe called Tony.

"What's up?" Tony asked.

"More detective work. We want you to come over for a think session."

"Okay. Incidentally, don't call Biff. He's here. We'll be right over."

Fifteen minutes later Biff's wagon wheeled into the Hardy driveway. The boys leaped out, took the front steps two at a time, and rang the bell. Joe let them in. Soon all four were deep in a discussion.

The Hardys told Tony of their discovery that the Flickering Torch was a restaurant.

"What's the strategy now?" Tony asked.

"Well, we've got two projects on our hands," Joe pointed out. "Recover the radioactive engine and investigate the Flickering Torch." He looked through the window. It was still raining, but not as heavy as before.

"Make mine the restaurant," Tony said with a wink.

"Double the order," joked Biff. "Tony and I are real rhythm hounds. We'll bring the whole band back with us if it'll solve the mystery."

Frank laughed. "I wish it were as simple as that. Anyway, it would help if you two checked out the place."

"What are we really after, Frank?" Biff inquired.

"I wish I knew, Biff. Just case the joint. See what you come up with."

"Maybe you can find out why Martin Weiss got fed up with the place," Joe added. "He must have had a reason."

Biff and Tony drove off with a promise to drop in at the Flickering Torch that evening.

The Hardys called Chet to give them a hand with the engine. They picked him up and set out for Marlin Crag Cliffs in the family car. It was drizzling slightly, but the wind had abated, except for an occasional gust.

When they arrived, Joe tied a rope to the bumper and tossed the other end to the foot of the cliff. Testing the rope to be sure it would hold his weight, he gingerly lowered himself over the edge. Dangling high over the rocks, he began his descent.

Suddenly there was a gust of wind and Joe veered crazily out into space. Then he careened back, hitting the stony wall with a thud that knocked the breath out of him. Frantically he clung to the rope, gasping for air. When he looked down, he could see a long drop onto the rocky beach.

"I'm a goner if I let go," Joe thought desperately. But his hands began to slip!

All at once his foot hit the cliff and came to rest on a narrow ledge. The toe hold enabled him to take some of the weight off his hands. Pausing until his strength returned, he climbed down the rope and jumped on to the beach.

Joe ran to the spot on the shoreline where they had left the engine. He kicked off his sneakers. Wading into the water, he looked around.

The engine was gone!

Joe returned to the foot of the cliff, climbed the rope to the top, and told Frank and Chet.

"Somebody must have taken it!" Chet exploded.

"There's a ledge along the shoreline," Joe stated. "The tide might have shifted it. Maybe the engine tumbled into deeper water."

"Another mystery to solve," Frank said, disappointed. He looked up into the sky. "It's getting dark already. We'd better head home."

That night the Hardys received a telephone call from the repair shop in Beemerville that their convertible was ready. They left the next morning by motorcycle to pick it up.

On Frank's Honda they zoomed past billboards and motels on the highway, and carefully moved with the traffic in small towns. Finally Frank sputtered to a halt at the garage.

They found their car looking as good as new. Frank loaded up the Honda, then slipped behind the wheel and drove into the street. He took the road linking up with the highway near the Marlin Crag Cliffs. It led up a steep hill toward the bluffs. After Frank crested the mountain, he started to descend.

Halfway down, something in the steering mechanism snapped. The steering wheel spun uselessly in his grasp as the convertible gathered speed down the incline!

CHAPTER VIII

The Emergency Exit

DESPERATELY Frank pushed the brake pedal to the floor. The convertible bucked and tires squealed, throwing the boys forward against their seat belts.

The car skidded sideways to the brink of a cliff. Hitting a big boulder, it tilted up on its left wheels.

"We're going over!" Joe shouted.

They braced themselves for the plunge. The car teetered toward empty space, rebounded on its four wheels, bounced a couple of times and settled in a cloud of dust.

Bruised and shaken, the Hardys climbed out.

"I thought for sure we were taking a long dive to the beach," Joe said weakly.

Frank's face was pale. "I'll never know why we didn't go over the cliff. This calls for some tall explaining at the repair shop."

The boys rode the Honda back to Beemerville and told the mechanic what had happened.

"Keep your shirt on!" the man replied to Joe's heated denunciation. "I don't know what conked out your steering mechanism."

The repairman had the car towed to the garage. While he was working on it, Frank and Joe stood by to watch. They knew quite a bit about mechanics and wanted to make sure that no one sabotaged the works.

"A loose connection," the mechanic said after he had found the trouble. "Just bad luck."

When he was finished, Frank gave the steering wheel and the brakes a good workout before trusting the convertible to the hill above the cliffs a second time. The boys shuddered when they passed the spot where they had had such a close brush with sudden death.

"Think our friend Mudd was behind the accident?" Joe asked.

"It's possible. He's our prime suspect," Frank replied.

After lunch Biff and Tony dropped in.

"Your staff is reporting back from the Flickering Torch," Biff announced with a grin.

"What kind of place is it?" Frank asked.

"Real jumping joint. Music is supplied by a hot combo called the Emergency Exit. We had a long talk with the drummer."

"He's a second cousin of mine," Tony added.

"His name's Bernie Marzi. What a surprise to see him there!"

"Did he say anything we can use in our case?" Joe wanted to know.

"Well, he said the place is managed by a guy named Leon Bozar. No one seems to know who the owner is." Tony balanced a coffee mug in the palm of his hand. "We hear Bozar's never around, though."

Nothing Biff and Tony had learned tied the Flickering Torch in with the plane crashes. But all four boys agreed to continue their investigation of the restaurant.

"We might get somewhere through the band," Frank said.

"That's easy enough," Tony stated. "Let me call Bernie." He phoned his cousin, explained that the Hardys were friends of his, and turned the instrument over to Frank.

"Hi, Frank," came Bernie's voice. "I've heard a lot about you and your brother and the cases you've solved. Anything I can do for you, just give the word."

"Thanks, Bernie," Frank said. "How about letting us have a rundown on the cast of the Emergency Exit?"

"Sure. There's Mark Bowen on the lead guitar, Linc Caldwell on the bass guitar, George Hansen on the rhythm guitar, and Pete Guilfoyle on the organ. Seymour Schill also plunks a guitar for us, and Joe Clark, a good friend of mine, is the em-cee."

"Tony and Biff say your combo's pretty good," Frank put in.

"We've almost always got a booking some-where," Bernie admitted. "And we've been play-ing at the Torch steady for quite a while. We do have a soft spot in our lineup, though."

"Oh? Who's that?"

"Seymour Schill. He's not too good."

"Why keep him?"

Bernie chuckled. "Finances, Frank. His father runs a music store and lets us have a lot of stuff for free. So we figure it's good business to let Seymour stick around."

They talked a while longer, and finally Frank said, "Thanks for the info, Bernie. We'll be see-ing you. Joe and I will drop in at the Flickering Torch tonight."

"Stop by the stage," the drummer invited be-fore hanging up. "I'll give you the big hello."

Joe telephoned Iola, who was eager to go out that night, and Frank made a date with Callie. They arranged to meet at the farm and drive to Beemerville from there.

Whey they arrived at the Mortons' place in the evening, the girls were ready.

"Where's Chet?" Joe asked Iola.

"He went to see an aviation engineer about getting some information on building his plane."

Joe grinned. "He's got a knack of finding the right people to help him."

Iola smiled. "He sure does. And he's arranged to take flying lessons."

The four climbed into the convertible and reached Beemerville without incident.

The Flickering Torch was a two-story roadside building with small wings flanking a medium-sized main building. Frank drove into the parking lot, where he stopped at the end of a row of cars facing a stone wall. The sound of music came drifting out into the night air.

"It's a popular dance place," Callie commented, "judging by the number of cars."

"The beat explains it," Iola said. "I feel like dancing already."

They entered a hallway and moved on to a large, dimly lighted main room, which was crowded with people. The emcee escorted them to one of many tables arranged in a semicircle around the edge of the dance floor.

At the rear was the stage on which the Emergency Exit was playing a popular tune. The floor was jam-packed with couples gyrating to the beat. Waiters passed bearing trays of food and drinks for those at the tables.

Psychedelic lights played constantly over the room, revealing faces in the crowd for an instant and then leaving them in darkness. Fantastic patterns cut across the walls and ceiling. Brilliant colors merged and separated in perpetual motion along the spectrum from red to violet. Flames appeared to be licking over everybody.

"I bet those lights are the reason why this place is called the Flickering Torch," Frank said. "Everywhere you look it flickers."

"Kind of spooky," Iola commented.

"Like Dante's Inferno," said Callie, who had recently done a paper on Italian literature. She looked around. Her eyes were getting used to the dim interior and the moving lights. "Do you see anybody you know?" she asked.

The Hardys carefully examined the faces of the patrons and shook their heads.

"I didn't think we would," Frank said.

Everyone ordered cokes. After downing the drinks, they paired off to dance.

Frank edged Callie toward the stage, where they paused just below the drummer. Frank recognized Bernie Marzi from Tony's description. After Bernie had ended a drum solo, Frank spoke to him in an undertone.

Meanwhile, Joe kept his eye on one of the guitarists, who seemed ill at ease, playing listlessly, and scanning the crowd all the time. At the intermission he hastened backstage.

"Iola, wait at our table," Joe said. "I'm going to follow that bird."

Affecting a casual air, Joe started for the door through which the guitarist had disappeared. He barely reached it when he bumped into the fellow coming back with another man.

Joe covered his embarrassment by pulling an envelope from his pocket and saying, "Excuse me, but I came backstage hoping to get your autograph."

"Sure," said the guitarist, who was about Joe's age. He was obviously pleased. Quickly he took out a pen and wrote *Seymour Schill* across the back of the envelope.

Joe threw a quick glance at Schill's companion. He was square-jawed, with a scar across the left side of his face. *Dale Nettleton!* The pilot who had almost hit their plane!

CHAPTER IX

Callie Plays a Trick

NETTLETON stared straight at Joe with hard, cold eyes.

"Does he recognize me?" Joe wondered. "If he does, he's covering up pretty well."

Seymour Schill handed Joe the autograph. He and the pilot then hurried through the door to the dining room. Joe shadowed them, keeping far enough behind to escape notice.

Schill disappeared outside. Nettleton went on the stage, bent over, and began fooling around with a tall cabinet amplifier. He seemed concerned about something at the back of it.

Suddenly he straightened up, jumped off the stage, and hastened out a side door.

As Joe moved forward to investigate, a group of young people swarmed across the dance floor in his path. He edged his way through them as fast as he could, but by the time he reached the door, his chances to intercept Nettleton had vanished. The flier climbed into a car and drove quickly out of the parking lot.

Joe returned to the table, where Frank, Callie, and Iola were waiting.

"Why the disappointed look?" Callie asked.

Joe sat down and quickly told of his encounter with Seymour Schill and Dale Nettleton.

"I guess Nettleton's one of the Marlin Airport group that hangs around the Flickering Torch," Frank commented.

"But Joe saw him doing something to the amplifier," Iola said.

"Would an ordinary patron do that?" Callie queried.

Joe shrugged and said, "Let's check on that amp, if we can, Frank."

At the next intermission Frank went up to the stage and returned with Bernie Marzi. He introduced the drummer to Joe and the girls.

Bernie sat down with them. "Enjoy the music?" he asked.

"We sure do," Callie replied. "It's great."

"Especially the drums," Iola added.

Bernie grinned at the compliment. "There's more coming up in about ten minutes. Put your dancing shoes on. The next number is a real wild one."

"By the way," Frank said casually, "is something wrong with your amplifier? If there is, I might be able to fix it for you. Amps are my hobby."

"Nothing's wrong as far as I know," Bernie replied. "But if you want to take a look, be my guest. Let me know if you find anything. I'm going to pop outside for a breath of fresh air before we begin the next number."

He nodded to the girls and left.

Frank leaned over and whispered to his brother. "I'll examine the amp, but I don't want Schill to see me. If he comes back unexpectedly, intercept him, okay?"

Frank walked across the dance floor and vaulted up onto the stage. He gave the amplifier an expert inspection, especially the part Nettleton had been fooling around with.

"Nothing wrong," he muttered to himself. "What can Nettleton have been up to?"

At the table, Callie was about to make a remark about Frank's puzzled look, when Joe grabbed her by the elbow. He pointed toward the door. Seymour Schill was just entering.

"Quick!" Joe urged the girl. "Do something to stop him before he sees Frank on the stage!"

Schill was almost at their table. Suddenly Callie stood up, let out a piercing scream, and collapsed against the guitarist, who caught her by the arms. But she managed to sink to the floor.

Callie lay on her back, quite still, with her eyes

closed. Schill dropped to his knees and began to fan her with a menu.

All the while, Iola wrung her hands. "Callie's unconscious!" she cried in simulated anguish.

Callie half-opened her eyes and squinted at Iola, who signaled her to get up. Frank was through with the amplifier and off the stage.

Callie rose shakily to her feet and brushed her dress.

Schill asked anxiously, "Are you all right?"

"Quite all right, thank you," Callie replied.

"What happened?" the guitarist wanted to know.

"A mouse ran over my foot!"

"No wonder you yelled," Iola said.

"We owe you a debt of thanks, er—?" Frank said, extending his hand.

"Seymour Schill's my name."

"Thank you, Seymour."

The musician looked pleased at all the attention he was getting. "Forget it," he replied. "I'm always glad to help a lady in distress. Especially a pretty one."

"Except for you," Callie put in, "I'd have a big bump on my head."

The group began to discuss popular music.

"The Emergency Exit has a terrific beat," Iola commented. "And you're so good!"

Seymour liked flattery. "I'm pretty far out," he

Callie pretended to faint

boasted. "It'll take the other guys a while to catch up."

"Any chance of us attending a practice session?" Frank asked in an offhand way. "We've got an amateur group and are interested in this sort of thing."

"Sure, why not? We hold rehearsals in a barn on Wednesday nights. Place owned by Pete Guilfoyle. You can come if you like. I won't be there next time, but the others will."

"Great!" Joe replied. To himself he said, "I wonder how this guy gets away with it. He's not too good anyhow and then he doesn't even show up for practice."

"I'll write down the address of the place for you," Seymour offered. He drew a printed card from his pocket and began to scribble on the back. Then a thought struck him. He turned the card over.

Frank and Joe, peering across his shoulder, read the legend: *O. K. Mudd's Airplane Junkyard, Main Street, Beemerville.*

Seymour put the card hastily back in his pocket. He began to look for something else to write on.

"Here, use this," Joe said, proffering a napkin. Seymour flattened it on a table, scrawled the address, smiled at the girls, and strolled over to the stage where the Emergency Exit was assembling. He began tuning his guitar.

"Our friend Seymour knows O. K. Mudd," Frank muttered.

"It could be strictly coincidental," Joe replied. "Mudd's got a big place and is probably known by most people in town. On the other hand there could be a connection between Mudd and the Flickering Torch, with Schill as a link."

"And if the Flickering Torch is in some way involved in the accidents, Schill definitely bears observing," Frank added.

The combo started playing a number. Couples drifted from the tables to the dance floor. The Bayport foursome joined them.

At the next intermission Bernie Marzi returned to their table. They engaged in some light chit-chat about music, then Frank asked if the drummer knew a Beemerville man named Mudd.

"Can't help you," Bernie replied. "Never heard of him. Should I?"

"Not unless you go in for used airplane parts," Joe replied.

Bernie laughed. "They're not my line."

"Is anyone in your group interested in that sort of thing?" Frank asked.

"Not that I know of."

Finally the band quit for the night. The lights of the Flickering Torch were dimmed and the patrons filed out into the night air.

Callie, Iola, Frank, and Joe settled themselves in their convertible. After a few miles of driving,

Frank flipped on the radio. He tuned it until the voice of a newscaster came through. The big story of the day made the boys sit bolt upright.

The announcer said, "A gang of thieves broke into a warehouse at Kennedy Airport earlier tonight in another bold freight heist. In a well-organized robbery, the gang overpowered the night watchman and transferred a whole consignment of air freight to trucks parked outside the warehouse.

"The trucks have vanished. The police are investigating, but Chief Reynolds admits that up to the time we went on the air, no clues to the gang or the stolen goods have been discovered."

The commentator turned to other news stories, his voice droning on.

Frank snapped the radio off. "That's a new development in Dad's case. He must be plenty upset about the gang's getaway."

"I wonder if he was close to nabbing them," Joe said. "Maybe the informer we're supposed to meet will give us a lead to this mob."

"All this is Greek to us," Callie said in a mock pout. "What's going on, anyway?"

Frank said, "We can't let you in on the details, but Joe and I may have a hand in catching that very same bunch of crooks."

"Do be careful," Iola pleaded.

"Don't worry," Joe said. "We always are."

The young people dropped into silence, busy

with their own thoughts as they rode along. Gradually a series of lights came into view on the right-hand side of the highway.

"That's Marlin Crag Airport," Frank informed the girls, "where Scott and Weiss were headed when they crashed."

Overhead, they could hear the motor of a small plane coming in for a landing. Suddenly the runway lights blinked off and on several times.

"Oh, look," Callie said.

"That's funny," Joe commented. "I've never seen that kind of signal to an incoming plane."

"There's something very strange going on," Frank said. "Joe, we'd better investigate this!"

CHAPTER X

Shots in the Dark

FRANK pulled the car over to the side of the road and switched off the headlights.

"We can observe the airstrip from here," he said. "I think something fishy's going on."

The control tower loomed in the distance, the muted lights from its windows brooding over the semidarkened field. Runway markers stretched out into the distance, and the strange blinking continued.

The airplane came closer and the young people craned to see it. Port and starboard lights were visible now, and the belly beam winked as the craft passed over them.

"Do you suppose the runway signal was meant for this plane?" asked Callie.

"Could be," Joe said. "Let's watch it."

Even though the pilot had plenty of runway, he failed to settle the plane down until near the end of the strip.

"Boy, I hope he doesn't overshoot!" Frank declared. As he spoke, the plane dropped several feet, then hit the ground smoothly with only yards to spare.

"Now what is he trying to prove with a landing like that?" Joe wondered as the plane turned about and headed back toward the airport buildings. The pilot taxied to an isolated shed next to a hangar, cut the engine, and stepped out. As he did, the lights stopped blinking along the airstrip.

"It certainly looks as if that signal was for him," Iola said.

Her words brought a chill of excitement to Joe. Could this incident have any connection with the metropolitan airport thefts? Was the plane carrying some kind of contraband? Why had it stopped at the isolated shed?

Joe mentioned his suspicions to Frank.

"Maybe it's only a wild guess," Frank said, "but you could be right."

"Then let's find out."

"What?" Iola said. "And leave us here?"

"That's a nice way to take two girls on a date!" Callie said in mock seriousness, but added quickly, "We understand. Go ahead. We'll wait for you."

Frank suggested that the girls drop them off and drive along the road until they found a good secluded spot.

"Pull in there and shut off the lights," Frank

said. "Joe and I have pencil flashlights. When we return we'll blink them once, then follow with three short ones. Be ready to pick us up. Okay?"

Callie giggled. "This is great, playing detective." She slid across to the driver's seat as Frank and Joe stepped out. They crossed the road and stepped down into a small gully which led to a low swampy area bordering the airport.

"Joe, look out, we're getting into some soft ground," Frank warned.

By paralleling the highway for a quarter of a mile, the Hardys avoided the swamp and pressed through high grass until they came to the edge of the runway. Both crouched down and looked about.

"If no planes come in for a few minutes, we can dash across the strip without being noticed," Frank said.

"All set?" asked Joe.

"Roger, keep your head low, and if anyone puts a light on us, hit the deck!"

The boys had taken no more than three strides across the runway when the sound of a twin-engine aircraft suddenly filled the air. They scrambled back for cover and lay flat in the grass, watching a passenger plane touch down smoothly. It reversed its engines, wheeled about, and taxied to the terminal.

"Okay, now!" Frank said.

He and Joe dashed across the runway and flopped prone in damp grass not more than a hundred yards from the shed. They listened tensely. Snatches of indistinct conversation drifted toward them.

"Let's get closer," Joe said.

Quietly they crept toward the building; then paused and raised their heads to get a better view.

Two men seemed to be getting the plane ready for takeoff. One stood near the wing with a fuel line, his back turned to the boys. The other walked to the rear of the plane.

"See what he's doing?" Frank asked.

"I can't make it out," Joe replied.

"He's working on the tailpost."

"Hey, he looks like Dale Nettleton!"

"Sh-sh," Frank warned. After a moment of silence he continued, "You're right, it *is* Nettleton. I wonder what he's up to now."

"Wait, here comes someone else," said Joe.

A short husky fellow in a pilot's uniform appeared from the shed and looked in the boys' direction. They ducked quickly.

Through stems of grass they saw the one man finish the refueling. Nettleton approached the pilot and they talked for a moment. Then the flier gave the thumbs-up signal and climbed into the plane. The starter whined, the propeller whirled, and the craft swung about to return to the runway.

Its noselight stabbed through the darkness as it

bumped its way over the rough ground to the blacktop strip. There it waited for a minute, obviously for clearance from the control tower, and took off into the night sky.

Nettleton and his pal hastened into the shed, and the Hardys stood up. "Well, what do you think?" Joe asked.

"Looked pretty suspicious to me," said Frank. "The pilot comes in and parks by a far-off shed. Then right away he takes off again."

"I wonder what's in that place," Joe said. They scanned the low building ahead of them. It had no windows, at least on the one side.

"Maybe those two guys in there are talking about illegal business," Joe said. "Let's try to eavesdrop on them."

Frank, glancing far across the runway and to the road on the other side, replied, "That's a long way to travel without cover. If they should spy us—"

"I think we ought to take the risk anyhow," said Joe.

"All right. But if you have any sneezing to do, do it now!"

Treading quietly, the Hardys approached the shed. They had gone no more than thirty feet when the door burst open and Nettleton stepped out. He switched on a powerful flashlight and caught the boys directly in its white beam.

"I thought I heard something out here!" he cried out. "A couple of snoopers!"

Frank and Joe stood speechless for a second, then turned and fled across the runway.

Two shots rang out behind them, which only served to increase the speed of their flying legs. The sudden sprint gave them a headstart on their pursuers, but the men were not to be shaken off that easily.

Shouts of "Halt! Stop! This is the law!" sounded behind them. Joe glanced over his shoulder to see two bobbing lights pursuing them.

"Head for the swamps!" Frank cried out.

"Why?" came Joe's breathless question.

"Because they're a lot older than we are, and will get tired sooner."

Joe followed Frank straight toward the swampy area. The tall stems of cattails loomed before their faces as they plunged through the wet ground.

"We've got them! We've got them!" Nettleton panted. "They'll never get through the muck!"

For a moment Frank doubted whether his tactic had been correct. Mud sucked and slurped at his shoes as he bulldozed his way through the marsh. Once Joe fell flat on his face, and Frank turned back to lend him a hand.

After scrambling another fifty feet, Frank whispered, "Let's stop for a second."

The boys crouched low in the muck like a couple of muskrats. They listened. There was no sound of thrashing now. Their pursuers were standing still, too.

"Do you see any sign of them?" asked Nettleton.

"Not a thing."

Frank and Joe recognized the voice immediately. *Bill Zinn,* the assistant airport manager.

A flashlight swept back and forth over the tips of the cattails.

"You think they got away?"

"I doubt it. They're playing possum."

"Then we'll flush them out."

"I told you we shouldn't have shot over their heads. I wanted to zap 'em!"

"None of that," Nettleton said. "They might be just a couple of skylarking kids. We'll find out soon enough."

The sound of sloshing feet began again. Joe rose to move on, but Frank restrained him. "Look, this is a big swamp," he whispered. "They might not find us at all. We can just wait them out."

"That's taking an awful chance," Joe whispered. The steps drew nearer.

"What do you see on your side?" came Nettleton's loud voice.

"Nothing," Zinn replied. "I can't make out any tracks, either. Let's go back."

"Nothing doing. We'll stick it out until we reach the road."

"Is Nick patrolling?"

"Right," Nettleton replied. "I've got him on the walkie-talkie."

"Okay, I'm with you."

The two forged ahead, each step bringing them closer and closer to the Hardys. Frank and Joe had flattened themselves in the muck, their chins pressed into the slime.

The men's heavy breathing became clearly audible.

"Good night!" Joe thought. "They'll be able to hear my heart beat!" It pounded with the excitement of danger.

The men took another step forward. Suddenly a heavy boot came down squarely on Joe's back. The boy let out a scream and jumped to his feet. Frank did the same.

Their double action stunned their pursuers momentarily. With an elbow thrust Joe knocked the wind out of the pilot, who had stepped on him. Frank's left jab caught Zinn flush on the chin. He fell over backward and lay still.

Without a word, Frank and Joe snatched up the men's flashlights.

By the time the two regained consciousness, the Hardys were well out of sight. All the boys could hear were curses behind them.

"We nearly got it that time," Frank said, pulling himself out of the edge of the swamp onto firmer ground.

"But we'll have to look out for Nick, whoever he is," Joe warned.

They tossed the big flashlights on the ground. Making their way in total darkness, the young detectives climbed the short embankment and reached the side of the road. Around a curve came two headlights. Frank and Joe ducked for cover again.

A car drove by slowly and a spotlight flashed across the marsh. But the cattails gave perfect cover to the boys. The car turned about and drove back toward the airport.

Minutes later Frank and Joe stood beside the road again, cold, wet and muddy, peering into the darkness.

"Lucky the girls are waiting for us," Frank said and took out his pencil flashlight. He gave a long beam, then three short ones. Several minutes went by, but there was no sign of the convertible.

An owl hooted in the distance, and the growl of an engine sounded as another plane took off.

"That's strange," Joe observed. "Why do you think the girls don't react?"

"I don't know," Frank replied. "Let me give them a couple more signals." He flashed the light again. Still no response.

"Good night!" Joe said worriedly. "Do you suppose something's happened to Callie and Iola?"

CHAPTER XI

No More Rocks

HAD the mysterious Nick come upon Iola and Callie in their hiding place? If so, the girls might be in danger!

Frank and Joe hastened along the edge of the road, giving the flashlight signal.

Suddenly, from a turnoff in the woods, a pair of headlights snapped on. For several seconds they glared into the darkness, then they went off, only to reappear in three quick blinks.

"Our signal!" Frank exclaimed, running toward the place of concealment. Joe followed him in full stride.

There was the convertible, backed into a clump of big bushes, between a stand of pine trees. Callie and Iola stepped out to meet the boys.

"Are we glad to see you!" Callie said, grabbing Joe's right arm with both her hands.

"Same here," Joe replied.

Iola said, "We thought you'd never come back! What happened?"

"Didn't you see our signal?" asked Frank. "You really had us worried."

"Of course we saw it," Callie answered. "But there was another car patrolling the road. We couldn't reveal our position!"

"Good thinking," Frank said. "We saw that car, too. Some guy named Nick was out to find us."

"Who's he?"

"He's part of the mob," Joe said as the boys climbed into the convertible. Briefly they told what had happened and pledged the girls to secrecy.

He slid behind the wheel and drove onto the highway, but instead of turning to the airport, he took the opposite route back toward Beemerville.

"Where are you going?" Iola inquired.

"This Nick might still be watching for us around the airport entrance," Joe replied. He explained that he would take an alternate route which would bring them into Bayport on a parallel road. After about three miles, Joe took a left turn and made a long detour to a secondary highway. He kept the car at speed limit all the way back.

The girls were let off at their homes with quick good-nights, then Frank and Joe continued on to Elm Street. The first floor of their home was well lighted.

Joe put the car away and the boys entered through the back door. They were faced immediately by their mother and Aunt Gertrude, who had waited up for them.

"Wherever in the world have you been?" Mrs. Hardy inquired with a worried look.

"A body can't get any sleep any more!" Aunt Gertrude complained. "Do you know what time it is?"

"Of course we do," Joe said, stifling a yawn with the back of his hand. "We were mixed up in a new development in our case. We just couldn't help being late."

"Looks as if you were mixed up in a mud bath," Mrs. Hardy said, the corners of her mouth relaxing.

"You're not kidding!" Frank kicked off his dirty shoes and set them beside the kitchen door. Joe followed suit.

"Aunt Gertrude, we're lucky to be back at all," Joe said. "We got chased, shot at, and—"

Aunt Gertrude wrung her hands, and an agonizing look crossed her face. "You're involved with gangsters again!" she wailed and turned to Mrs. Hardy. "Laura, it's too dangerous for these boys to play detective!"

"It wasn't any play, I can tell you that!" Frank observed as he stripped off his mud-spattered sport shirt.

"Here, give me those dirty things," Mrs. Hardy

said. "I don't want you to trail mud into your room."

"Thanks, Mother." Joe grinned.

Gertrude Hardy clucked disapprovingly. "Well," she said, "at least we can all go to bed now. Frank, Joe, mind you're up in time for breakfast and church!"

The next day was Sunday. Early afternoon Sam Radley dropped in and discussed the latest turn of events. After the Hardys had told him everything that had transpired the day before, Frank concluded, "That assistant at the airport, Bill Zinn, is a prime suspect."

"So are Mudd and Nettleton," Radley added. "They should be investigated."

"That's where you could help us," Joe put in. "Could you start checking on Zinn? You know what I mean—his background and all that?"

"Be glad to."

"Great," Frank said. "Meanwhile, we'll go back to Mudd's place and do some further sleuthing there."

After Radley had left, Joe said, "What do you have in mind about the airplane junkyard, Frank?"

"We need to follow up that tailpost clue. Remember Chet's fuselage? The tailpost was missing."

"Now I get it," said Joe, snapping his fingers. "Last night Nettleton was working on the tailpost of that plane. Maybe something was hidden there!"

Frank nodded and Joe went on, "What's your strategy?"

"I really don't have any yet," Frank replied. "We could ask Chet— Wow! That gives me an idea. Come on!" Frank went to the telephone and dialed the Morton farm.

Chet answered. "Hello, Frank. You're lucky to find me in. I was just practicing loops."

"Oh, good," Frank said. "Are you ready for an Immelmann yet?"

"Ha, you can't stump me," Chet said. "Isn't that the outside loop invented by that German ace?"

"Let's get back down to earth," Frank said. "There's something I'd like you to do for us."

"Listen," Chet said, "my pilot's training can't be interrupted by—"

"Come on," Frank urged. "All we want you to do is ask Mudd for a tailpost."

Silence for a moment, as Chet mused. "Come to think of it, I could use one, too. And maybe some other parts. Okay, it's a deal. When do we go back to Beemerville?"

"Tomorrow. And listen, Chet. We want you to wear a bug."

"Come again?"

"A bug—a concealed microphone," Frank explained. "Stick close to Mudd; this way we might pick up a clue. Since he knows you're building a plane, that gives you a good excuse to hang around a while. We'll be listening in all the time, so you don't have to worry."

Chet joked, "Where are you going to put the bug? In my ear?"

"Never mind, we'll take care of that," Frank replied. "We'll pick you up in the morning."

When Frank hung up, Joe smiled. "Pretty good thinking, Frank. What kind of a bug is it going to be?"

"A medal to hang around his neck," Frank said. "Oh, and I want to call Tony, too. We might learn something more from a meeting with his cousin Bernie."

"You mean about the Flickering Torch?"

"Right."

Fortunately Tony was at home, too. "Sure, I can get Bernie down here," he said. "I'll arrange it as soon as possible."

The Hardys spent the rest of the afternoon working on a miniature radio pickup. They concealed it in an ornamental medal which they attached to a chain.

"Chet'll look real cute in this," Joe said. "That is, if he'll wear it."

"He will," his brother replied.

Next morning at the breakfast table Joe came up behind Aunt Gertrude and put the medal around her neck. "My goodness, what's this?" she asked.

"Oh, just a little something to show you our appreciation," Frank said with a wink at Mrs. Hardy.

"Why, what's it for?"

"All you have to do is sit and talk to Mother for a few minutes," Frank said. "We'll be right back."

"I'll bet they're up to something again," Aunt Gertrude said as the boys exited through the back door.

Frank ran to the car and got a receiver. "Listen to this," he said to Joe.

Aunt Gertrude's words along with Mrs. Hardy's came through clearly.

"Well, what's on the agenda today, Laura?" asked Aunt Gertrude.

"The laundry, the upstairs bathroom, all the upstairs windows, and the coat closet," Mrs. Hardy replied cheerfully.

Aunt Gertrude sighed. "You know, as fond as I am of the boys, sometimes I wish they were girls and would give us a hand with the housework!"

Frank grinned as he recorded the conversation. Then the boys returned to the dining room.

"Frances and Josephine Hardy checking in," Joe said. "Wow, you can't imagine how glad we are to be boys!"

"Detective work is much more fun than cleaning out the coat closet," Frank added. He set the recorder on the table and played back the conversation.

"Oh, you scallywags!" Aunt Gertrude exclaimed. "You shouldn't eavesdrop like that!"

"Well, we had to test the bug!" Frank said, and took the chain off Aunt Gertrude's neck. "See you later."

They hurried out of the house, got into their car, and were soon at the Morton farm. Chet was waiting for them.

Joe handed him the medal.

"Where's the bug?" Chet asked.

"You're holding it," Joe replied. "Drape it around your neck."

Chet grinned and did as he was told. "How do I look?"

"Just beautiful," Joe replied and gave him a sharp rap on the arm.

Frank drove to Beemerville and parked several blocks from the Mudd Airplane Junkyard. As prearranged, Chet walked up to the main gate alone. As soon as he disappeared, Frank and Joe quickly approached the metal fence that surrounded the junkyard.

The boys set their receiver and adjusted the tape, then turned to a crack in the sheet metal.

"Chet doesn't seem too happy about his mission." Joe chuckled as the receiver transmitted a nervous gulp from their hefty pal.

"Oh, oh, here comes Mudd," Frank said.

The man strode out of his office and confronted Chet. "What do you want now?" he demanded in an irritated voice.

"I'm looking for a tailpost, Mr. Mudd," Chet replied.

"A tailpost!" Mudd said with a look of astonishment. "What for? You don't even have a fu—"

The man stopped in confusion and his face turned red. Chet pounced on the blunder like a cat after a ping-pong ball. "Oh, I got my fuselage back, Mr. Mudd," he said in an offhand manner. "Some clown swiped it and dropped it at a garbage dump. I found it later. So I'm back in business for some airplane parts. A tailpost, please."

Mudd's eyes narrowed threateningly. "Look, where're your pals?"

Chet said coolly, "I couldn't really guarantee where they are."

"Oh, yeah?"

"Come on, now, Mr. Mudd. I want to look around at some parts. You can see I'm alone, can't you? Now how about a tailpost?"

Joe whispered, "Chet's doing a great job!"

Mudd began talking again. "I don't have any to fit your model fuselage."

"That's too bad," Chet said. "Well, I'll be

needing wings later. Mind if I check around to see what's here?"

Mudd gave a sardonic laugh. "You'll need wings all right, you fat brat. And a harp, too!"

He moved toward Chet. Grabbing the boy's arm, he twisted it around his back in a hammer lock. "I've stopped fooling with you," Mudd snarled. "Where are those buddies of yours, and what are you snooping around for?"

Joe tensed and made a move to spring up. Frank held him back. "Wait! Chet knows how to take care of himself."

Their friend's short gasp of pain was followed by a rebel yell. Chet put his experience as a high school wrestler to good use. Swinging his body around, he flung the heavier Mudd over his back. The man hit the ground with a thud, then rose shakily to his feet.

Chet confronted him in a wrestler's defensive stance, feet wide apart, hands extended forward. At the same time he noticed that the chain had slipped over his head and fallen onto the ground.

"We'll lose contact," Joe hissed.

"Maybe not," Frank said. "Look!"

A young man entered the junkyard. It was Seymour Schill! He bent over and retrieved the bug. Swinging it by the chain, he looked from Chet to Mudd.

"Cut the rough stuff, will you," he said. "Who's this kid you're muscling?"

"I'm no kid!" Chet said indignantly. "My name's Chet Morton, and if this gorilla wants some more action, I'm ready for it!"

"Don't get physical," Seymour said. "I've got nothing against you. I just want a few words with O. K."

He drew the man aside and spoke in a voice too low for Chet to hear. However, the bug dangling in his hand picked up every word.

"The boss has made up his mind," Seymour said. "It'll be Wednesday and Saturday."

"Good," Mudd responded. "That suits me just fine."

"Same time, same place," Seymour went on. Pausing for a moment, the guitarist added significantly, "Same number of rocks."

"No!" Mudd's voice was harsh. "Tell him no more rocks, understand!"

"I understand. What's the pitch?"

"Hard cash from now on!"

CHAPTER XII

Jam Session

THEIR conversation finished, Seymour and Mudd turned to Chet again. Seymour tossed the medal at him.

Chet caught it on the fly and pulled it quickly over his head, vastly relieved that Seymour had not examined the medal closer.

"Chet's heading back for the car," Joe observed through the crack in the fence.

"Good. We've made some headway," Frank said. "Let's join him."

The Hardys assembled their receiving apparatus, slipped quickly around the fence, and made tracks for their convertible.

Chet arrived shortly afterward. "Did you see? I almost got conked!" he began excitedly.

"We saw," Joe said. "You were great, Chet!"

"We also heard everything," Frank added. "Our

little bug worked like a charm. And Seymour couldn't have done us a bigger favor!"

"When he picked it up I thought I was sunk!" Chet declared, rolling his eyes. "What did they say?"

Joe repeated the conversation.

"Interesting, but what does it mean?"

"We don't know," Frank said.

"That talk about rocks," Chet went on. "Suppose they meant the Marlin Crag Cliffs?"

"No. Precious stones, perhaps. Remember, Mudd asked for hard cash—another kind of payment."

"And what about Wednesday and Saturday?"

"Well, something's going on then, but we don't have any idea what or where."

"The Flickering Torch is my guess," Chet said with a professional air.

"Possible," Joe agreed. "We'll have to watch the place."

The trio returned to Bayport, still puzzled about the overheard clues. Next afternoon Tony Prito and Bernie Marzi showed up at the Hardy house.

After a hearty welcome by Frank and Joe, Bernie asked, "What can I do for you? Tony mentioned a case you're involved in, but didn't give me any details."

"We can't tell you too much either," Frank said. "But you could help us by telling us everything you know about the Torch employees. Something suspicious may be going on there. We'll have to check out the place. How about starting out with the musicians?"

"Sure," Bernie said and gave a short summary of everyone's background. "I know very little about the waiters and the kitchen personnel," he concluded. "As far as the band goes, I trust everybody with the possible exception of Seymour Schill. I can't tell you why, it's just a hunch."

Frank nodded slowly. "Your intuition and ours are surprisingly alike."

"What's the next step?" the drummer asked.

"We'd like to case the Flickering Torch," Joe stated.

"Listen, I've got a great idea!" Bernie exclaimed. "Why don't one of you join the combo Saturday night? Who handles the lead guitar?"

"I do," Joe said. "What about your regular guitarist? Won't he be jealous?"

"He wants the day off, Joe. We were going to hire another pro. But I'm sure you can fit the bill, so why should we look for anyone else?"

"I'll take you up on that, Bernie. When do I have to be there?"

"First you'll have to attend our practice session tomorrow. Let the gang see how you do."

"Suits me fine," Joe said. "I've always wanted to play with pros."

Tony grinned at Bernie. "That means Joe'll

have a jump on the rest of us in the Bayport combo."

"Never fear, we're not that good," Bernie said modestly.

When Tony announced he would have to leave in a little while, Joe asked Bernie if he was planning to return to Beemerville that evening.

"No," Bernie replied. "I'm supposed to spend the night at Tony's and go back tomorrow."

"Listen," Joe suggested, "why don't you stay here and then we can drive down together?"

"Have you got room for me?" Bernie asked.

"Sure."

"Hey, that's great," Bernie said. "Especially since I don't have a car."

"It's a deal. Let me tell Mother." Joe hastened upstairs and returned with Mrs. Hardy, who offered Bernie their hospitality. Then Tony departed.

A few minutes later the phone rang. It was Mr. Hardy.

"Where are you, Dad?" Frank inquired.

"Morrisville, New Jersey," the detective said. "At the airport. I've tracked the hijacking outfit this far. Now I need some help."

"We'll come double-quick, Dad. But there's a new angle at this end. Joe'll tell you about it."

He handed the phone to his brother, who hurriedly described his plan to join the Emergency Exit, so he could keep an eye on the Flickering

Torch and its patrons. "What should I do?" Joe concluded. "Cancel out the music?"

"Not at all," Mr. Hardy replied. "Go ahead with your surveillance. All I need here is Frank."

The dark-haired boy took over again. "Sure thing, Dad," he said. "Give me the orders."

"I can't over the phone," Fenton Hardy told him. "Come to Morrisville late tomorrow afternoon and we'll talk it over. I've got a job at the field as a porter, so it'll be easy for us to meet without arousing suspicion."

"Anything else?" Frank queried.

"Well, Sam Radley's still checking on Mudd's record. So far there's nothing about Zinn. That's it for now. Take care, both of you."

The following day Frank decided to let Joe and Bernie have the car. After an early dinner, they dropped him off at Bayport Airport, where he got a commercial flight to Morrisville, then the two went on to Beemerville for their practice session.

They reached the area in a little more than an hour.

"Sure is pretty country," Joe remarked as Bernie directed him off the highway. They drove along the coast road. The Marlin Crag Cliffs now gave way to sandy beaches which swept inland in a half circle. In the middle of the broad curve lay a small fishing village called Pohasset. It was a little past Beemerville and was frequented by artists who haunted the wharves and scenic dunes.

Stretches of green marshes were dotted with small houses and outbuildings.

"See the house up on the knoll?" Bernie asked.

"The one with the barn near the waterfront?"

"Yes," the drummer remarked as Joe slowed down. "Pull in the drive. That's Pete Guilfoyle's place where we hold our jam sessions."

Joe parked the car under an elm tree and got out to look around. The barn lay about two hundred feet from the house, nearly at the water's edge. Its front doors stood open, revealing an unusual interior.

It certainly was not for horses. Instead, an organ stood on the right side, and chairs were scattered about, along with two amplifiers.

"Nice place to practice, eh?" Bernie said. "We can vibrate it apart and nobody complains."

Joe's eyes were following the shore as he walked toward the barn. He noticed a boat rocking in the water some distance away. Concealing himself behind a tree, the boy looked intently at a man standing up in the boat. The fellow had binoculars and the late-afternoon sun glinted off the polished lenses.

"Bernie, take a look at this," Joe said.

"The guy in the boat?"

"Yes. I think he's spying on us."

"Oh, he's probably just a bird watcher," Bernie said. "Why would he be interested in us?"

The man in the boat sat down, started an outboard motor, purred a little farther away from the shore, then stopped to scan the barn once more.

"We seem to be the birds he's watching," Joe mused. As he spoke, two more boys drove up in their cars. Bernie introduced them.

"Joe, meet Linc Caldwell and George Hansen," he said. "Fellows, this is Joe Hardy, who'll sub for Mark Bowen this weekend."

"Okay with us," said Pete, who had just walked down from the house. "We're with you, Joe, as long as you can play the guitar."

Joe grinned. "Try me. But say, there's something I want to get straight before we start." As the boys entered the barn, he walked over to the first amplifier to check it out. It looked normal. He did the same to the second.

"Not a thing out of kilter," he muttered. "I wonder why Dale Nettleton was fooling around the amp at the Flickering Torch."

"Dale Nettleton? You know him?" Pete asked.

"Casually," Joe replied. "What about you?"

"Oh, he hangs around the Flickering Torch. Always interested in the band."

Bernie, who had been holding Joe's guitar, pushed the instrument into his hands. "Okay, Joe, let's hear some sweet sounds!"

The Hardy boy got in line with the other guitarists. Bernie sat just behind them. Under Pete's direction, the beat started low on the drums. The organ picked up the theme, weaving in and out in an intricate pattern. Then came Joe's lead guitar in a short, burbling pizzicato. The rhythm guitar supported the tune, succeeded by the bass.

Then it was Joe's turn again. At first he was a little hesitant, but soon the music was vibrating through his body. He began to cut loose, improvising wild harmonies, an octave higher than the bass guitar.

The sound reverberated from the rafters. The amplifier swayed as the combo came up to a crescendo, hit the final notes, and ended the first piece. Bernie Marzi looked over from his drums.

"Joe!" he called. "You're great!"

Pete Guilfoyle added, "Want a permanent job with us?"

"You're a lot better than Seymour Schill," Linc Caldwell said.

Joe grinned. "Nice of you to ask me, fellows, but I'm not really in your league yet. Well, how about another piece?"

As the music soared again, faces began to appear in the doorway. Local people were congregating to hear the Emergency Exit rehearse as they always did, tapping their feet and clapping their hands to the tempo.

After the walls of the barn had trembled for more than two hours with the pulsating vibrations, the rehearsal ended. The young musicians joked as they packed their instruments and Pete Guilfoyle approached Joe.

"Nice going. We're glad to have you with us."
He glanced at his watch. "It's getting pretty late.
Are you planning on going back to Bayport to-
night?"

"I suppose so."

"That's a long way. How would you like to
sleep in the barn loft? I'd invite you inside, but
there isn't enough room."

"That's a good idea," Joe said. He stepped
aside and said to Bernie, "That fellow in the boat
might show up again in the morning. Maybe I
can find out what's cooking."

"Good," Bernie said. "See you Saturday."

Joe thanked Pete for the invitation.

"Don't mention it," the boy replied. "You'll
find blankets in the loft. Make yourself comfortable. I'll turn off the lights and see you in the
house for breakfast, okay?"

"Fine."

Joe climbed the rungs of the ladder and pulled
himself up to see a pile of hay and several blankets.
He wriggled into the dry grass.

While drowsiness overcame him, Joe pondered
the stranger in the boat. Soon he was fast asleep.
In his dream he watched the man start his motor.
It exploded with a giant *boom*, causing Joe to
sit bolt upright.

Outside, thunder was cannonading along the
shore, and through a small window he saw great

streaks of lightning. These were followed by a tor-
rent of rain.

The door creaked open. Then, caught by a gust
of wind, it slammed shut violently. Joe got to his
knees, crawled to the edge of the loft, and looked
down.

Lightning flashed again and for a moment he
could not see anything. Then, in the shadows, he
made out the figure of a man!

The fellow listened, then moved stealthily toward the ladder leading to the loft!

CHAPTER XIII

Lefty the Squealer

THE intruder glanced up and Joe pulled back out of sight. Had he been seen?

The boy listened, his heart pounding with excitement. All he could hear was a *drip, drip, drip*. The roof leaked, and droplets of rain splashed on the ladder. Perhaps that's what had caught the man's attention! Joe fervently hoped so.

No other sound now. Joe craned forward cautiously. The shadow was moving toward the door. It opened quietly and the stranger disappeared into the night.

"I'd better trail him," Joe decided. He hastened down the ladder. It was wet from the rain. Joe's feet slipped. His sagging weight was too much for fingers that clutched the slick rung above him. Down he went!

Joe fell heavily to the barn floor, striking his head against the post supporting the loft. He lay stunned, for how long he did not know. When he opened his eyes again, there was an eerie silence in the barn. The rain had ended and the trickle from the roof no longer splashed on the ladder.

Joe rose to his feet and rubbed a bump on the back of his head. Then he stepped to the door, opened it quietly, and looked outside. The landscape was bathed in silvery light, cast by a full moon which shone pale between fluffy clouds.

The boy followed the path leading to the road, moving at a crouch and searching for possible clues which the intruder might have left. But the rain had obliterated all tracks. By the time Joe reached the edge of the road, he knew the man had made a clean getaway.

Suddenly he noticed a small shiny object on the ground. He reached down in the gravel and picked up a plastic guitar pick. Was the night visitor a musician?

Joe pocketed the pick and walked back toward the barn, still alert to possible danger. If the prowler were one of the fellows in the band, why had he come back? Or could it have been the stranger in the boat, who had been spying on the Guilfoyle property?

Joe was about to enter the barn when he heard the sound of an approaching motor. A vehicle was driving up the road slowly.

Joe ducked, dropping on his knees behind a bushy azalea plant. He watched. Out of the darkness appeared a large van. The words MOBILE X-RAY on its side were visible in the moonlight. The driver stopped in front of the barn. The cab doors swung open and two men jumped out. They peered around, then went into the barn.

Joe listened, pressing his ear against the wall. There was a sound of scraping metal, then footsteps as the men came out again.

A voice said, "One more contact and we're finished."

"Things are getting too hot around here," the other man replied. "It's just as well."

Pondering what it all meant, Joe watched the men as they returned to the van. They climbed in, and the doors slammed.

Joe reached for his car keys. They were not in any of his pockets! "I must have dropped them in the barn," the boy thought desperately. "Now I can't follow these birds!" Suddenly he had an idea.

He sprinted from his hiding place and dashed toward the road, just as the van started off in first gear. As the vehicle picked up speed, Joe ran behind it, looking for a handhold. Nothing was accessible except the bumper.

Joe grasped it with both hands, then swung his feet up under the chassis, resting his heels on the muffler. If he could only hold on until the van stopped!

But Joe had not bargained with the exhaust pipe. It emerged near his face, sending out a hot

Joe grasped the bumper with both hands

stream of carbon monoxide. Joe turned his head away from it, sucking in gulps of air and trying to hold his breath as long as possible.

Finally, however, a numbness began to creep into his hands and he wondered if he should drop off. The noxious fumes made the decision for him. Joe fell unconscious to the road like a sack of potatoes!

If Frank Hardy had known what was going to happen to his brother, he would not have gone to his assignment in New Jersey so eagerly.

Once Frank had arrived at the Morrisville airport, he picked up his suitcase from the baggage claims center and headed toward the exit, where a porter sidled up to him and grasped the handle of his bag.

"May I help you with this, young fellow?" the porter asked. "It's kind of heavy."

"No thanks. I'll carry it myself," Frank replied with a sidewise glance at the man. Then a big smile came to his face. "Okay, you can take it, Dad."

"Not so loud," Mr. Hardy cautioned. "And get that grin off your face!"

"Where'll we meet?" Frank asked as they advanced toward a line of taxicabs in front of the terminal.

"I made reservations for you at the George Washington Motel. It's only a few blocks from here on the road leading into town. I'll see you there at six," Mr. Hardy said.

It was a happy reunion between father and son that evening.

"I'm glad you came," Mr. Hardy said. "Remember I told you how informers operate?"

Frank nodded. "Sure. You pay them off and they squeal on their own grandmother."

"Right. Informers are like double agents. But they make out very well, unless they're caught."

"And then what?"

His father made a motion across his throat. "It's too bad for them. That's why we must be very careful."

"So you found an informer?" Frank inquired.

"Just by luck." The detective told Frank that he had trailed a truckload of stolen merchandise from the New York airport, but had lost track of it in the vicinity of Morrisville.

"I figured they must be flying the stolen freight out of here," Mr. Hardy concluded.

"But how did you latch on to the informer?" Frank persisted.

Mr. Hardy said that he had checked in with the local police. They had had an anonymous phone call about something phony going on at the airport. The tipster left a number which proved to be a public telephone booth and said he would give them the details for a certain amount of money.

"Did they pick him up?" Frank asked.

"No. They didn't have enough cash in their budget," Mr. Hardy replied. "When they told me, I decided to take the chance. The freight insurers gave me carte blanche."

"Have you seen the man?"

"No. He calls himself Lefty and agreed to meet my contact on the southeast corner of Broad and Market streets in Newark, exactly at eleven forty-five tonight. I want you to deliver this to him. It's the money he wants." Mr. Hardy pulled out a fat envelope from his jacket pocket.

"How'll I know this Lefty character?" Frank inquired.

"You won't. But he'll know you."

"How?"

"You'll mop your brow with this every now and then." Mr. Hardy handed his son a blue handkerchief. "Frank, this is a dangerous assignment," he went on. "You pay Lefty the money, and he'll give you a message. Get it straight. You might not even have time to repeat it."

"Don't worry, Dad. I'll pay strict attention," Frank said.

Father and son had supper in the motel restaurant, then Frank took a bus to Newark. He arrived on the corner of Broad and Market shortly before rendezvous time. The movie theaters had emptied minutes before, and traffic was moderately heavy.

Frank took his place at the designated spot, and

smiled to himself. "I feel kind of silly doing this," he thought as he reached for the handkerchief. He mopped his brow several times looking around in the crowd for some kind of recognition. After a while he noticed a man on the opposite corner staring at him. He appeared to be in his late twenties, thin, with bushy dark hair.

Frank mopped his brow again. The fellow casually sidled across the street, then walked up close to Frank.

"Lefty?" Frank asked.

The man nodded. "Follow me."

Keeping several paces behind, Frank followed the man east on Market Street, where he stopped before an all-night restaurant. The smell of cooking wafted on the warm air through the open facade.

Lefty jerked his thumb indicating "inside," and led the way to the back, past long counters crowded with people who had stopped for a quick hamburger or hot dog with sauerkraut.

There were three vacant tables near the rear exit. Lefty pulled a chair for himself and motioned Frank to sit down.

"We'll get this business over with right quick," the informer began. As he spoke, three men walked past them to one of the remaining empty tables. Frank barely noticed them, concentrating instead on his companion.

"Okay," Frank said. He produced the envelope

and handed it to Lefty. The latter opened it, pulled out a roll of bills, counted them and put them into his pocket. Then he bent close to Frank.

"Get this," he whispered. "Die . . ."

What came next happened so quickly that Frank was completely taken by surprise. One of the men at the other table sprang out of his chair and dealt Lefty a karate chop at the back of his neck. Then the assailant and another man grabbed each of the unconscious man's arms and began to drag him out the back of the restaurant.

"Hey, wait!" Frank said as he started toward the prostrate figure of Lefty. But the third man, a barrel-chested fellow, barred the way!

CHAPTER XIV

Sky Chase

FRANK backed off into a defensive judo stance. Out of the corner of his eye, he noticed a fourth man sneaking toward him from behind.

The young sleuth spun on his heel and lunged forward, putting all his weight into a perfect football block that threw the man backwards. A table splintered as the thug crashed onto it and slid to the floor.

Frank dashed past and ran out the front door. He saw a walk alongside the building and hastened to the dark alley behind the restaurant, hoping to catch up with Lefty and his captors. But he was too late. Nobody was in sight.

Frank trotted back to Market Street and looked up and down in vain for the informer or the four assailants. His attention was drawn to a ragged bum with a bushy beard who trudged along the sidewalk with the aid of a bamboo cane. He stopped when he saw Frank. Then he painfully inched his way forward, and sidled up to the young detective.

"Pal, can you let me have a quarter for a cup of coffee and a doughnut?" he whined.

Frank fished in his pocket, brought out a coin, and handed it over. "Old-timer, maybe you can do something for me," he suggested.

A crafty look crept over the hobo's face. "Is it worth another quarter?"

"Well, I'll give you the two bits anyway," Frank said, delivering the second coin. "Now, did you see three men come out of the restaurant a few minutes ago?"

"Not me," said the man, clutching the money in his fist. "But I don't see much around here. It's safer not to."

As he spoke, a car careened to a stop at the curb. The husky driver got out and jumped on Frank. The two hit the pavement and rolled over in a violent free-for-all. The assailant caught Frank's head in the crook of his powerful right arm and applied crunching pressure.

Frank gasped for air. Bells sounded in his head and black spots flickered before his eyes. His senses reeled.

Suddenly he saw the bum go into action. Raising his cane, he brought it down on the man's head with a resounding crack. The fellow keeled over with a glassy stare.

Frank staggered to his feet. "Th-thanks," he gasped. "You've got some wallop to kayo that gorilla."

"You didn't know it was me," said a familiar voice dryly. The old vagrant stood up straight. His stoop disappeared. He pulled off his bushy beard.

"Dad!" Frank exclaimed. "How do you happen to be here?"

"I thought I'd better tag along on this mission," Fenton Hardy said. "I tailed you while you were tailing Lefty. They've got him all right. Pushed him into a car and drove off."

A moan came from the man who had jumped Frank. Fenton Hardy grasped him by the collar and hauled him to his feet, while Frank ran to get a policeman. Half an hour later they were at head-quarters.

The sergeant at the desk recognized Frank's assailant immediately. "A strong-arm for hire. He's got a record as long as Broad Street."

After advising the man of his rights, the sergeant said, "Okay, want to talk?"

"I got nothing to say," the man growled. "I want to see a lawyer."

"That's your privilege. But we're holding you for assault on Frank Hardy."

Father and son returned to Morrisville in a rented car to spend the night at the George Washington Motel. The detective explained that he had been afraid Lefty would double-cross him.

"I was worried about that, too," Frank said. "But poor old Lefty was okay. He was talking to me when they clobbered him."

Frank told his father about the word "die" just before the attack.

"Lefty could have meant somebody was about to be rubbed out," Mr. Hardy said. "And it might be me!"

Frank shuddered. "Dad, we'll have to be extra careful on this case! The freight thieves have a neat racket. They'll do anything to keep it from blowing up in their faces."

Next day Frank found no difficulty in getting a job in a car wash at the Morrisville Airport. His task was drying the cars as they reached the end of the cleaning line. From this station he could easily watch the planes landing and taking off.

About noon Frank's surveillance brought results. He spotted Dale Nettleton coming out of the Midatlantic Distribution Corporation office. The pilot carried a suitcase, which he carefully deposited in a small plane. After that, he went back to the office and stayed inside for some time.

Frank made a snap decision. Taking advantage of his lunch-hour break, he hastened to the terminal for a quick conference with his father, who was still posing as a porter.

"Nettleton's taking off somewhere, and he

seems awfully concerned about his suitcase," Frank said. "I'd like to see what's in it. We might have the goods on him, Dad."

"What's your plan, Frank?"

The boy looked out through the broad plate-glass doors of the terminal. "Nettleton hasn't come out of the Midatlantic office yet. I may have time to hire a plane and follow him!"

"Good idea. But watch out. He's probably crafty."

"Okay. Will you straighten things out with my boss over at the car wash?"

"Sure. And good luck!"

Fenton Hardy went to help a passenger with some bags, while Frank trotted off to hire a small plane. He had just completed the transaction when Nettleton emerged from the office. He quickly got into his airplane and taxied away.

Frank had to wait for runway clearance, which allowed time for Nettleton to become airborne without suspecting he was being tailed. Then Frank followed him into the sky.

Checking the vector Nettleton was traveling, the boy saw they were heading for Marlin Crag Airport. "Same route the pilots took before they crashed into the cliffs," he noted ominously.

Frank kept his eyes fixed on the plane ahead, determined not to lose his quarry. But in doing so he drew closer and closer to the lead craft.

Nettleton suddenly became suspicious and took

evasive action, curving to one side to let his pursuer go by. Frank did the same.

Nettleton turned upward, gaining altitude in a burst of power. So did Frank. At last Nettleton went into a steep dive and pulled up sharply. A collision seemed imminent. In a desperate move, Frank shoved the stick forward and made a tight diving turn.

His plane screamed past Nettleton's without a foot to spare. The green pastures below him spun as Frank fought to bring the plane under control. Finally he managed to level out.

He resumed tailing Nettleton, who by now was little more than a moving speck between fleecy white clouds.

As he was closing the gap again, Frank tuned into the Unicom frequency to pick up anything his quarry might broadcast. He heard Nettleton's voice in a frantic appeal for help. "Listen, buddy, get this Hardy brat off—"

Frank chuckled. "He must be rattled. Ought to know I might be listening in!"

The Unicom frequency went dead. Frank knew Nettleton had realized his mistake.

A few minutes later Marlin Crag Airport came into sight. Circling into the approach from the sea, Nettleton lifted his plane above the cliffs and came in over the airstrip. The craft bounced hard several times before effecting a landing.

Frank made a three-point touchdown without a

tremor, and taxied to a stop near Nettleton's plane. Seeing the pilot take the suitcase and rush into the terminal, Frank jumped out and ran after him. Nettleton went into the Marlin Crag office of Midatlantic. Frank followed.

The pilot swung around. "You bother me, wise guy," he snarled. "And that's a quick way to get hurt."

"Why so edgy, Nettleton?" Frank asked. "You got something to hide?"

"That's none of your business!" the pilot fumed. "Don't push me!"

"Level with me and I'll lay off," Frank promised. "I've been watching you, and my guess is you're up to something. I just might blow the whistle on you."

"What's the charge?"

"Maybe receiving stolen property. Like hijacked air freight."

The pilot's face darkened. He gave Frank a venomous glance. "Where did you get that crazy idea?"

"Could be your suitcase," Frank replied.

"My bag's got nothing to do with you," Nettleton snapped.

"How about opening it then? Or is it filled with gold bricks from Fort Knox?"

"Okay, smart aleck, take a look," Nettleton said furiously.

Opening the valise, he turned it over, allowing

the contents to spill out on the floor. Frank saw the usual things that would be in an overnight bag—shirt, socks, shaving equipment and so on.

"Found anything incriminating?" Nettleton sneered.

Frank lifted the suitcase. He ran his hand around the interior, searching for a hidden compartment. He rapped the sides, tugged on the straps, and examined the nameplate. Finally he set the bag back on the floor.

"I hope you're satisfied!" Nettleton stormed.

CHAPTER XV

Dangerous Contraband

FRANK was chagrined at finding nothing important in the suitcase. A look of satisfaction came over Nettleton's face as he replaced the clothing and toiletries. The flier was one up on him now!

Frank thought fast. Hoping to throw Nettleton off balance, he said, "I'm almost satisfied, but not quite. I'd like to inspect your engine!"

Nettleton looked startled. He was stammering a bit over his answer when the office door opened and Bill Zinn walked in.

"Oh, it's you, Hardy," Zinn said. "What brings you here?"

Nettleton said, "This guy thinks there's something wrong with my engine. He'd better forget it!"

"Don't fly off the handle, Dale," Zinn said quietly. "There's no reason why Hardy shouldn't look at your engine."

He motioned Frank to the door, and the three walked across the concrete apron to the edge of the runway where Nettleton's plane was parked.

"Zinn seems awfully sure of himself," Frank thought as the manager handed him tools to make the inspection.

The young detective checked the tailpost and found it in order. Then he scanned the engine and paused when he came to the vacuum pump. He went over it carefully.

"What's bothering you?" snarled Nettleton, who watched Frank's every move like a hawk.

"Is there something about that vacuum pump you don't like?" Zinn asked sarcastically.

"It's okay," Frank replied. "But I know one pump housing that was as empty as Bayport beach in February."

Frank's reference to Jack Scott's engine with its missing vacuum pump had the desired effect. Both men stiffened and became stony-faced. Frank knew he had scored. Zinn and Nettleton were connected with the airport fatalities in some way!

"Well thanks, fellows," Frank concluded, handing the tools back to Zinn.

"Don't mention it," the manager said icily. "Is there anything else you'd like to inspect around here?"

"That'll be all," Frank replied.

Nettleton and Zinn exchanged glances as Frank walked off. He knew they were worried. He also realized that the airport should be kept under constant surveillance. Something fishy was going on. If enough eyes watched every movement at Marlin Crag, it might come to light.

Frank stepped into a phone booth and dialed Bayport. Joe answered.

"Hey, Frank, where are you?"

"Marlin Crag Airport."

"How'd you get there?"

"Flew up from Morrisville in a rented plane. But listen, Joe, I'll tell you all about that later."

"Have I got a hairy story for you!" Joe said. "But it'll have to wait. What's up?"

"I don't have any concrete evidence," Frank stated, "but Nettleton and Zinn seem to be involved in those crashes." He told what had happened and suggested that Joe help him stake out the airport.

"I've got an even better idea," Joe replied. "Those fellows from the band are swell guys. I'm sure they'd come too if I'd ask them."

"All right. Get in touch with them. What about the guys in Bayport?"

"They're all helping Mr. Prito on a construction job and Chet's too busy matching wings with the Red Baron."

About two hours later Joe Hardy pulled into the airport with Bernie Marzi, Linc Caldwell, George Hansen, and Pete Guilfoyle.

Frank, who had kept an eye peeled for their

convertible, hastened up and shook hands with everyone.

"I want you to know that I gave up a date with a real cute chick to come here," Pete announced.

Frank grinned. "That's greatly appreciated." He took the boys aside behind a row of parked cars, where he told his suspicions regarding Nettleton and the aircraft.

"I really didn't expect them to let me see the engine," Frank said. "After all, why should they? But Zinn seemed almost eager for me to look at it. I think if we spy on them and the plane, we might find out what's cooking."

Frank and Joe assigned lookout posts. Dusk had fallen and partially concealed the young men as they took a circuitous route through the airport grass toward the edge of the runway.

"Keep your heads low," Joe advised as they went to their places.

When it was completely dark, the Hardys inched up close to the edge of the runway. Fortunately the grass had not been cut for a while and provided good cover.

Frank and Joe heard excited voices from the same shed where they had eavesdropped the other night. Then two men walked out with flashlights and approached the plane.

"Why didn't you tell me earlier that they were missing?" said one of them, whom the boys recognized as Nettleton.

"I didn't have a chance to check all afternoon," replied the other man, who was Zinn. They hurried past the craft for several hundred yards along the runway, then stopped. Their flashlights bobbed about like fireflies in July.

"They're looking for something," Joe whispered.

Frank recalled the hard landing of the plane. Had a piece of the undercarriage broken off? Was that what the men were looking for?

Now the searchers got down on their hands and knees.

"It must be something small," Frank surmised.

"Oh, oh, look what's coming," Joe said.

In the distance the landing lights of a plane blinked on, beaming down onto the runway. The men scrambled out of the way, running only a few feet past the place where the Hardys were concealed.

"Forget it," Nettleton said. "We're not going to find them in the dark. We can look again in the morning."

"All right," Zinn agreed. "And next time, if you can't make a better landing, get somebody else to do the job!"

The plane touched down and taxied to the terminal. The men had disappeared and Frank rose, giving a small quiet whistle to attract the others. They crowded around him.

"Something was lost on that runway," Frank

said. "Come on. Let's go and look for it ourselves."

Frank and Joe carried pocket flashlights. All six hastened to the spot recently vacated by Nettleton and Zinn. They hunkered down and examined the concrete surface.

After a while Pete said, "Nothing here that I could see."

"What are we looking for, anyway?" asked Linc.

"There's something!" Bernie exclaimed suddenly and picked up a gleaming object. "A piece of glass!"

"Here's another one," Joe said. He cupped both glinting pieces in the palm of his hand and shone the light on them.

"I don't think they're glass," Frank observed.

"Well, they couldn't be diamonds!" Bernie said emphatically.

"Why not?" asked Joe.

George Hansen chuckled. "In that case I'll take my share and buy a new guitar."

Joining in the levity, the boys had not noticed two men running toward them.

"Look out!" Pete warned suddenly.

"Run!" Frank cried out.

George, Bernie, Linc, and Pete took off through the high grass. Frank and Joe brought up the rear. As the men raced up, the Hardys stopped short, spun around, and sent their surprised pursuers crashing to the ground with a judo assault.

Then the boys put on a burst of speed and

caught up with the others at the car. They all piled in and Frank took the wheel.

"We shook 'em off all right," Linc said. "What happened?"

"We discouraged them," Joe remarked. "I think those stones we found must really be diamonds or they wouldn't have come at us like that!"

"We'll find out for sure and let you know," Frank promised.

After thanking the young musicians, he dropped them off at their homes and the Hardys sped back to Bayport. They arrived to find their father waiting for them.

Everyone sat down at the kitchen table, and Joe described his adventures at the Guilfoyle barn. He concluded with the episode on the mobile X-ray van. "I must have rolled off while it was taking a curve," Joe said. "I landed in a ditch and woke up with a horrible headache."

"Did you ever find the car keys?" Frank asked.

"Yes. They were in the barn."

Mr. Hardy said, "I doubt that it was really an X-ray van. Probably some sort of coverup for an illicit scheme."

"What do you think the racket is?" Frank asked. "Do you have any theory about the van?"

"Not yet."

Frank described what had happened at the airport. The boy took the two stones from his pocket and handed them to his father. The detective looked at them absently, still mulling over Frank's question about the mobile X-ray van.

"I've discovered something about rays," Mr. Hardy revealed. "I contacted the Atomic Energy Commission after you told me about Scott's radioactive engine. They told me there's some radioactive contraband in this area!"

"What?" said Joe. "Contraband—what kind, Dad?"

"Uranium isotopes!"

"The stuff that goes into the atomic bomb!" Frank gasped. "Is someone making an atomic device?"

"Not necessarily. Uranium isotopes have a lot of uses. But the smugglers are using them illegally, according to the AEC."

"Where are these isotopes coming from?" Joe inquired.

"England is the suspected point of origin. Scotland Yard is working on the case in London. And I wish we could crack it at this end."

"Is there a tie-in with the Marlin Crag plane crashes? Did Scott's vacuum pump housing become radioactive because of uranium isotopes?"

"Quite possibly," his father replied.

"Maybe Mudd figures in the racket, too," Joe said.

"Sam Radley's checked him out," Mr. Hardy stated. "He has broken the law a few times, but they were only minor infractions. If he's mixed up with contraband isotopes, he's going big time. Sam has no information to indicate that."

The detective turned his attention to the stones in his hand, got a jeweler's loupe from his desk drawer, and examined them minutely.

"They're manufactured diamonds," he said finally. "You can see they were made by the industrial method of subjecting carbon to high pressure and high temperature in a lab. Take a look."

"But how do they come into the case?" Joe asked.

"Maybe that's what Lefty was going to say!" Frank exclaimed. "I thought 'die . . .' meant somebody was going to be rubbed out. But it could have been diamonds."

"Hey, Frank!" Joe said excitedly. "Remember the conversation between Seymour Schill and Mudd when Chet was at the junkyard?"

"Wow! You're right. Mudd said 'No more rocks. Hard cash from now on.' Maybe these are the rocks!"

The phone rang. Frank answered, then turned around. "It's for you, Dad."

An unfamiliar voice on the other end of the line caused the detective to frown. A man asked, "You Hardy the fuzz?"

"I'm a private investigator, if that's what you mean," the detective replied evenly.

"Well, you better take your investigatin' some place else."

"Who is this speaking? Please identify yourself."

"Never mind who I am," the caller said. "All you got to know is that we've caught Lefty."

"Where is he?"

"That's our secret."

"Is he all right?"

"Yeah, but he won't be if you don't lay off!"

"What do you want?"

"You been givin' us a lot of trouble, Hardy. Me and my pals don't like it. We'd be obliged if you'd stop leanin' on us."

"And if I refuse?"

"There goes your stool pigeon. It's a fast trip to the bottom of the bay for Lefty next time you give us any trouble. Think it over."

The phone went dead. Mr. Hardy relayed the conversation to his sons. "I'll have to play it cool," he said thoughtfully. "Lefty's life is at stake."

"Joe and I can carry on," Frank suggested.

"Okay, but you'll have to be very careful," Mr. Hardy said, looking proudly at his sons.

The next day Frank and Joe were busy with various chores at home. Early Saturday morning the phone rang and Joe answered. After a brief conversation his face fell and he hung up.

"What's wrong?" Frank asked.

"That was Pete Guilfoyle," Joe replied. "His combo has been fired by the Flickering Torch!"

CHAPTER XVI

False Alarm

"THAT's a switch!" Frank exclaimed. "The Emergency Exit has had raving reviews in the papers. How come they got the boot so suddenly?"

"Pete doesn't know. They played last night, and when they were through Bozar told them not to come back. Joe Clark, the emcee, got sacked, too."

"I'll bet the gang thinks the fellows know too much," Frank said. "They were probably recognized at the airport Thursday night."

"And Bozar's in with the gang," Joe added. He looked glum. "My first job with a red-hot professional combo and it blows up in my face."

"Maybe not, Joe. I have an idea."

Frank put through a phone call to Bernie Marzi, who confirmed that the Emergency Exit had been fired.

"Tough luck, Bernie," Frank sympathized.

"But maybe it's good luck for us. I suppose the Torch will be looking for a replacement?"

"Sure."

"Well, how does this sound to you? We've got a pretty good combo here in Bayport. Suppose we apply for the job?"

"Brilliant idea. If you're all as good as Joe, you'll be a big hit. Contact Arthur J. Mulholland in Beemerville. He's the agent."

The Hardys summoned Phil Cohen to do the talking. He came over in ten minutes and telephoned the agent.

Mulholland seemed pleased. Yes, the Flickering Torch needed a band immediately, he said. What a coincidence. He was checking through his files at that very moment. "And I don't have a folk rock group on tap!" he concluded.

"Search no further, Mr. Mulholland," Phil said confidently. "I have a great band that's available."

"What's it called?"

Thinking quickly, Phil came up with a name. "The South Forty," he answered.

"Never heard of them," the agent replied.

"They're big around Bayport," Phil assured him. "Three guitars, drums, and organ."

"What's your name?"

"Phil Cohen."

Mulholland asked some technical questions about music. Phil expertly fielded every one of them.

"Okay, you seem to know your stuff," the agent said at last. "I'll give you a shot at it. You'll start tonight. Leon Bozar, the manager, will pay you."

"We'll be there with our gear," Phil promised.

"Okay, but don't bring any amplifiers. The manager of the Flickering Torch says they use only their own. They have an organ, too."

Phil thanked the agent and hung up. Joe let out a whoop of triumph.

"Great going, Phil. From now on you're our agent."

The Hardys contacted Biff and Tony. Biff offered to drive them all in his father's station wagon.

"Good," Frank told him. "We'll meet at our house about seven-thirty. We're due on stage at nine o'clock sharp. And by the way, Biff, Joe and I will wear disguises so don't panic when you see us!"

While waiting for evening, Frank and Joe decided to use the afternoon to make an aerial search for the mysterious van that Joe had seen at Pete Guilfoyle's place. They drove to the airport for their plane and Frank piloted the craft north along the coast. He flew in from the sea and drifted lazily over the Marlin Crag Cliffs. Then he circled low over Beemerville, where the Flickering Torch stood out clearly on the highway.

"See anything exciting?" Frank asked as he turned past Beemerville.

"Lots of cars, trucks, and trailers, but no big van," Joe replied.

"Negative here, too. I'll head back for Marlin Crag. The woods are bigger there. Good place to hide a vehicle that size."

The cliffs loomed up on their horizon again. They saw the surf below pounding against the rocks and hurling spray high in the air. Frank flew out to sea and then back.

Suddenly Joe nearly jumped out of his seat. "I see it, Frank!" he exclaimed. "That van down there between the trees at the end of the lane! It's the same shape and color as the one I hitched a ride on."

Frank dived down and circled low over the vehicle. On the side of the van, gleaming in the sunlight, were the words: MOBILE X-RAY.

"No doubt about it now," Frank agreed. "That's the van we're after!"

He headed toward the airport and asked the control tower at Marlin Crag for clearance. When he received it, he came in for a quick landing. After parking their craft, the boys raced to a car-rental office. Within minutes they were speeding toward the woods.

Joe was at the wheel. He turned off the highway onto a dirt road, the wheels picking up a cloud of dust. Reaching the lane, the car jolted into an open space and careened to a stop.

The place where the van had been was empty!

"It's gone," Joe said.

"Have we got the right location?" Frank asked.

"I'm positive."

"Then it might be somewhere near here," Frank said. "We'll cruise till we find it."

Joe swung the car around and they roared back along the dirt road, bouncing along and scouting the woods as they went.

Suddenly Joe cried, "There it is!" He stepped on the brakes and pointed up a side path where a big vehicle was parked facing them. The driver had raised the hood and was tinkering with the engine.

Joe drove straight to the spot and parked, facing the van, bumper to bumper. "This guy isn't going to make any sneak getaway," he muttered. "Unless he can fly that van over us!"

As the boys jumped out, the man lifted his head. He was thick-set and had a rugged face.

"Hold everything!" Frank ordered.

"What's this all about?" the driver asked in surprise.

"We'd like to know what you've got in your van," Joe told him.

"What's it to you?"

"Just say we're curious," Frank said.

"The police might be interested, too," Joe added.

The man turned pale.

"Do we get to inspect the van, or don't we?" Frank pressed.

The man shrugged. "I guess I can't stop you. Go ahead."

Frank and Joe ran around to the rear of the vehicle. Each grabbed a handle and swung the doors open, then stared at a cargo of tables, chairs and other household furniture.

Embarrassed, Frank looked at the name on the side—MIDWEST MOVING COMPANY.

Joe gulped and turned red. "Frank, I made a mistake."

"You can say that again," Frank replied, then turned to the driver who had followed them.

"Sorry, sir," he apologized. "We thought you might be a crook."

The man looked relieved. "Believe me, I was afraid you were a couple of shakedown hoods. Now that I've fixed the engine, I'll be on my way."

The Hardy boys went back to their car. "Am I mortified!" Joe confessed.

"You and me both," Frank said with a rueful grin.

They cruised around for a while longer without spotting the van they were after. Frank, who was driving now, finally turned back to the airport. "It's time to head for home," he noted.

The psychological letdown was hard to overcome and the boys felt tense that evening as they put on their disguises. Mrs. Hardy and Aunt Gertrude looked on as Frank and Joe fixed cheek pads and eyebrows and donned wigs. Frank put on a false mustache.

"I do hope you'll stay out of danger," Mrs. Hardy said nervously.

"Nothing good can come of these disguises," Aunt Gertrude added. "Gracious, you frighten me!"

"Don't worry," Frank assured the women. "There'll be five of us at the Flickering Torch. We can take care of ourselves."

Biff drove up in his father's station wagon with Tony in the front and Phil in the back seat. The Hardys stowed their guitars in the back and slipped in next to Phil. The South Forty rolled north toward Beemerville.

They were surprised when they were met by Seymour Schill at the door of the Flickering Torch. Schill showed no recognition of Frank and Joe.

"I'm the emcee for tonight," he proclaimed. "I'll announce your program. But first," he added with a self-important air, "you'll have to do a warm-up number so I can see if you're good enough for us."

The Bayport youths played one of their favorite pieces. Seymour seemed impressed. "You'll do," he said when they had finished. "Let's start the program. The patrons are arriving."

The band played for about an hour, doing renditions of songs that had the listeners tapping their toes and snapping their fingers to the varied rhythms. A dance melody led up to the first intermission.

Seymour came over and had a big smile on his face. "Say, gang, you're great!" he said. "Come along. A lot of patrons are dying to meet you."

"I'm not sure we should," Frank said. He glanced about for any sign of Nettleton or Zinn.

"You've got to be kind to your public," Seymour insisted. "That's part of being in show biz."

Unable to come up with a plausible refusal, Frank led the way down to the dance floor where a crowd was milling around. Each member of the band was promptly buttonholed by a music fan.

An effusive blond teen-ager engaged Frank in conversation. "I think your combo is too sweet for words," she cooed.

"Er—thank you," said Frank, who had his eye on the stage. Dale Nettleton had just come in and was tinkering with the amplifier!

Frank tried to edge away but the girl linked her arm in his. "Do tell me what you're playing next," she begged.

Desperately Frank went through the program. "Now if you'll excuse me, I'll have to get ready," he said.

"That's the only reason I'd accept," she said archly. "Keep the rhythm coming my way!"

Frank looked back at the stage. Nettleton had vanished. Quickly the boy walked up and checked the amplifier. He found nothing wrong with it. When the band tuned up, the amp carried the sound without distortion.

"What *is* Nettleton up to?" Frank asked himself. But there was no time to mull over the question. The music began again. The South Forty zoomed through some melodic country rock before shifting into a louder beat.

They hit a deafening crescendo at the end of the last piece. The floor shook. The windows rattled.

And then the amplifier fell over with a terrific thump! What looked like the magnet fell off the back and rolled across the stage!

CHAPTER XVII

The Payoff

THE audience applauded at the end of the program, clapping their hands and stamping their feet. The five Bayport youths bowed.

"Fellows, I have an idea we're a hit," Phil said out of the corner of his mouth.

"They dig us," Tony agreed.

But Joe hardly noticed the applause. "I can't wait to see what fell off the amp," he murmured.

As the audience drifted away, he leaped forward and pounced on the object. The rest of the combo gathered around him.

"It's a lead cap," Joe commented, "and not really part of the amp!"

"What's it for?" Biff inquired.

"Look here," Joe said. He picked the amplifier from the floor where it had fallen and placed the cap over the magnet at the back.

"A perfect fit," he said. "The magnet holds it in place."

Tony whistled softly. "No wonder the amp was top-heavy!"

Frank nodded. "That's what fooled me when I inspected the amp. I thought the cap was the magnet."

"I still don't know what that hunk of lead is for," Biff persisted.

Frank shrugged. "A lab test should give us the answer," he said. "We'll take it home to Bayport and find out."

"You're not taking anything to Bayport!" a voice interrupted. The boys turned to see Seymour Schill advancing with a scowl. "All right, hand it over!"

"Hand over what?" Joe asked in feigned ignorance.

"That chunk of lead. Give it here!" The guitarist reached out suddenly in an effort to snatch it from Joe.

But Joe was too quick for Seymour. He lobbed the piece underhand to Frank. When Seymour rushed at him, Frank made a sidearm toss to Biff Hooper. Seymour leaped forward again, only to have Biff flip the piece of lead back to Joe. This infuriated Seymour, who screamed his defiance.

Sensing something was amiss, some of the patrons of the Flickering Torch rushed toward the stage to gawk.

In the midst of the turmoil, Frank's false mustache fell off. Frantically he tried to press it back, but no luck. What was worse, somebody identified him!

"Hardy!"

Frank glanced in the direction of the shout and saw O. K. Mudd pushing through the crowd.

"That's Frank Hardy!" Mudd shouted. "I recognize him without his phony mustache! Grab him, Seymour!"

"Grab him yourself," Seymour retorted. "I can't handle all of 'em!"

"You introduced a bunch of spies!" Mudd's voice was hoarse with anger. "You numbskull, you let the Hardys trick you!"

"What do you want from me?" Seymour protested, his eyes bulging in frustration. "Mulholland hired them. Not me. I just took it from there."

"Never mind." Mudd stopped short of the group and regained control of himself. "At least we know who they are. The party's over!" He turned to Frank. "I want that piece from the amplifier!"

"Why should we give it to you?" Frank asked.

"Because it's not your property, that's why."

Phil asked, "Whose property is it?"

"It belongs to the Flickering Torch."

"Then it's not yours either," Biff pointed out, "unless you own the place!"

Mudd flushed a deep red. He looked around as

Joe lobbed the lead cap to Frank

if searching for help. Suddenly he broke into a smile. A husky policeman approached. His hair was whitish blond and he had a slight limp.

"What's the beef about?" he inquired.

"Officer," Mudd complained, "the Hardy boys and their cronies are stealing club property."

"Like what?"

"A piece of the amplifier."

"Let me see it!" the policeman ordered.

Joe came forward and handed him the chunk of lead. "It's not a piece of the amplifier," he said. "We suspect that something illegal is going on here and suggest that this be checked out in the police laboratory."

The officer stared at him angrily. "Cut the baloney, kid," he growled. "What are you trying to do, play FBI? I've got a good mind to arrest you. Get out of here while you're still in one piece!"

He turned and gave the lead cap to Mudd, who accepted it with a triumphant smirk.

"You Hardys stay out of my way from now on," he threatened, "or you'll wind up under a slab in my junkyard!"

As the policeman left, Mudd and Seymour went off the stage together, talking in low tones.

"Well, how do you like that?" Biff exclaimed in disbelief.

"That cop didn't even listen to us!" Tony complained.

"That piece of lead must have been worth an awful lot to O. K. Mudd," Joe mused. "Too bad we couldn't have a better look at it."

Frank placed his guitar in its case. "Well, let's take the policeman's advice and get out of here. I think he *would* run us in if he had the chance."

The five youths were walking toward Biff's station wagon when Frank suddenly handed his guitar to Joe.

"We haven't been paid!" he exclaimed. "I'm going back inside to see Bozar. I'll meet you at the car in a few minutes."

At the front door Frank noticed Mudd and Seymour entering the manager's office behind the dance hall. "I'd better find out what those two are up to," he thought. He sneaked through a clump of small trees and reached the rear of the restaurant. He ducked down and scrambled along the wall until he reached a lighted window in the far corner. Sounds of voices came from within.

Very slowly Frank raised his head and peered over the sill. A broad desk stood at one end, facing a sofa at the other end. Two easy chairs flanked the sofa.

Mudd was sitting in a swivel chair behind the desk. Seymour Schill stood on the opposite side, facing him. The junkyard proprietor opened a middle drawer and took out an envelope, which he handed to Seymour with the words, "Here's your dough."

The guitarist removed a bundle of bills from the envelope and counted them.

"What's wrong?" Mudd snapped. "Don't you trust me any more?"

Seymour snickered as he put the money in his breast pocket. "Trust you? After that little episode with the band? You've got an idea I let you down with the Hardys. So I wanted to be sure you didn't short-change me."

"The Hardys?" Mudd snarled. "Forget them. They won't be bothering us any more. From now on it's business as usual for you and me."

"Okay, Mudd," Seymour replied. "But don't get ratty with me again. I don't like it."

The pair walked out of the office, Mudd turning off the lights at the door.

As Frank stood up to leave, a dry leaf crackled behind him. He whirled around in time to catch a glimpse of the policeman creeping up. The man's nightstick flashed out and a gigantic Roman candle exploded in Frank's head. Then he crumpled to the ground in blackness.

When Frank came to he was bound hand and foot with rope. He sat up and looked around.

Frank was in a small laboratory painted white. Fluorescent lighting threw a glare over the interior. Along one side, rows of shelves held bottles of various sizes. The opposite wall was lined with scientific instruments and small metal containers, many of lead. A table covered with test tubes and electronic equipment stood at the far end.

A low moan caused him to turn his head. Another prisoner lay near him. The man moved convulsively, revealing his features.

Lefty the informer!

He looked haggard. His eyes were tightly closed. His lips twitched.

"Lefty!" Frank gasped. "What's going on?"

"He can't hear you, I'm afraid," said a smooth voice.

Frank twisted around and saw a man in a white coat. He was carefully filling a hypodermic needle with a whitish fluid. With a sinister smile he said, "Lefty couldn't care less about what's going on."

"Well, I care!" Frank snapped. "Where are we?"

"Come, come, Hardy, you know enough science to recognize an experimental laboratory. Splendidly equipped, don't you think?"

"What kind of experiments are you carrying out?" Frank demanded.

"They concern the radioactivity of subatomic particles."

"Uranium isotopes," Frank guessed.

"Precisely."

"Who are you?"

"Dr. John Weber. I'm quite distinguished in the field of physics, if I do say so myself."

"Why are you telling me all this?" Frank asked suspiciously.

"Because the information will die with you," Dr. Weber said with a leer.

He advanced toward Frank, holding the hypodermic syringe in his left hand. The fingers of his right hand toyed with the plunger. The long needle gleamed wickedly!

CHAPTER XVIII

Diamond Dust

BACK in the station wagon, Joe fidgeted nervously. "I wonder what's keeping Frank," he said.

Phil shrugged. "Maybe Bozar's trying to weasel out of the deal."

Joe flicked on the radio and they listened to music for a while. Fifteen minutes went by. Still no sign of Frank. Joe glanced at his watch.

"That's long enough!" he decided. "Something must have happened. I'm going back."

"We'll come with you," Biff offered.

All four left the car and strode into the Flickering Torch. They found the place vacant except for employees who were cleaning up after the evening's entertainment.

One man pushed a broom over the dance floor, while another stuffed scrap paper and soda bottles into a bag. Waiters were carrying plates and glasses into the kitchen.

Joe asked about Frank. None of the employees had seen the boy return!

Suddenly Biff grabbed Joe's arm. "Look! There's Seymour!" He pointed to the guitarist, who was just about to leave the building.

"Hey, Seymour!" Joe called out. "Wait! Have you seen Frank?"

Schill stopped and faced the boys. "Last time I saw your brother, he was up at the stage with the rest of you. Meanwhile I thought you all had gone home!"

"We came back to collect our fee," Phil said pointedly.

"Didn't Bozar pay you?"

"No."

"He's left already. But maybe the check's on his desk. I'll look."

Seymour disappeared into the manager's office and returned shortly.

"Here it is," he told Joe and handed him a check made out to the South Forty. Then, with a tired wave of his hand, he left.

"Let's search inside," Joe said as he pocketed the check, "then we'll scout the grounds."

Phil and he took the main floor. They looked behind the stage and in the kitchen, finally examining the rest rooms and the check room.

Biff and Tony found their way to the cellar, which was filled with cases of soda and cartons of restaurant supplies.

"Frank, where are you?" Tony called. No reply. The four met again after a fruitless search.

"Let's try outside," Joe said. He ran to the car and returned with two flashlights, then the boys circled the Flickering Torch. Their investigation of a garage behind the building revealed nothing, neither did the bushes, hedges, or the gully across the road from the restaurant.

Now the last of the lights were winking out. Joe played his flashlight against the window of Bozar's office. Directly beneath the sill, the beam picked up a small flower bed. Zinnias and marigolds lay crushed into the soil.

"Look here," Joe said. "Footprints! Two sets of them!"

"Frank was probably trying to look inside," Phil said, "when somebody jumped him."

"And he was knocked down and carried off to a car waiting at the road!" Tony conjectured. "Now what'll we do?"

"Call the police," Joe said without hesitation. "But first I want to get in touch with Dad."

The boys returned to the car and drove along the road until they found a telephone booth. Joe put in a call to Bayport. He got his father and quickly told him that Frank was missing.

"A dangerous turn of events," Mr. Hardy said. "Call the authorities. I'll meet you at the State Police Barracks in about an hour."

As planned, they rendezvoused at the barracks,

where Lieutenant James Cook, a tall wiry man, was told about Frank's disappearance.

"We'll have to question everybody connected with the Flickering Torch," he said. "Can you give me any leads other than the footprints beneath the window?"

Joe spoke up. "There have been several mysterious things going on around here." He told of the elusive van and added, "If Frank was kidnapped, that might be a good place to hide him."

"We'll check it out," Cook said, and ordered his men to set up a dragnet for the van.

"Anything else?" he asked.

"Yes. I think Mudd's airplane junkyard should be searched, too," Joe said. "He threatened that if we didn't lay off, we'd wind up under a slab in his junkyard! Frank might be held prisoner there!"

The lieutenant was intrigued and asked for full details of the Hardys' case. Joe and his father quickly related all the developments in the mystery from the time they had taken on the airport investigation up to the point where the policeman had snatched the lead cap which had fallen from the amplifier.

The lieutenant nodded thoughtfully. "One thing is clear from your description of the policeman," he said. "It doesn't fit any of our people in this area, be it state or local police. He probably was a phony."

"I think you're right," Tony added. "That fake cop must be a crony of O. K. Mudd."

"I'll get a search warrant for Mudd's place," Cook said. Then he instructed one of his assistants to broadcast a seven-state alarm for Frank Hardy, describing the young sleuth in detail.

The boys looked exhausted after their work at the Flickering Torch and the excitement that had followed.

"Why don't you all go back to Bayport?" Fenton Hardy suggested. "You won't be able to help at this point. Joe can stay here with me, and if we need the rest of you, we'll give you a call. Okay?"

Phil was about to protest, but then saw the logic in the detective's reasoning. After a quick good-by, the boys drove home in Biff's station wagon.

Joe and his father presently fell asleep in their chairs until Lieutenant Cook woke them up.

"It took some doing at this early hour, but I've got a warrant to search Mudd's premises. Want to come along?"

"Sure do," Mr. Hardy replied, rubbing his eyes.

The lieutenant, two of his men, and the Hardys drove directly to Mudd's home. Joe and the detective waited as the junk dealer was routed from bed. He came to the door, bleary-eyed and angry. "What's this all about?" he grumbled.

Lieutenant Cook showed the warrant. "This is for the search of your property, Mr. Mudd. Frank

Hardy is missing and we have reason to believe that you're holding him."

Mudd gave a nasty laugh. "You're crazy. Go right ahead and look all you want. I've got nothing to hide."

The troopers searched the house first. Then they took Mudd to his junkyard.

"This is ridiculous!" the man protested. "I don't know anything about that Hardy kid!"

He glared angrily as the two policemen searched his office. But again there was no sign of Frank.

As they were about to leave the building, Joe spied a pipe-like object standing in one corner of the office. It was an airplane tailpost. The boy pointed to it and said, "Lieutenant Cook, I suggest we examine this!"

"Keep your hands off it!" Mudd stormed.

Cook, however, picked it up. He turned the tailpost on end and a narrow container fell out. Joe grabbed it and hit it lightly against his palm. A tiny glassy splinter dropped out.

"Hey, give that to me!" Mudd cried. He made a lunge for Joe. Before Mr. Hardy or the police could restrain him, he hit the boy two heavy blows, knocking Joe down. Instinctively the young detective made a tight fist and held on to the splinter.

"You're under arrest!" Lieutenant Cook thundered as his men seized Mudd. They quickly subdued him and handcuffed him. Then they led Mudd to the patrol car.

Though groggy, Joe rose to his feet and said, "Lieutenant, I have a hunch that this splinter from the tailpost might give us a clue."

"I'll have it tested in the lab," Cook said.

After a thorough search of the junkyard proved futile, they all drove back to the barracks, where Mudd was booked on a charge of assault and led into the holdover cell.

Cook said, "I think we're on to something important. Mudd is really worried about what Joe found in that tailpost."

In the laboratory Cook himself put the splinter under a high-powered microscope. He focused the lens, took a long look, and raised his head.

"Well?" Mr. Hardy inquired. "What did you find?"

"Looks like a diamond splinter to me," the lieutenant replied, shaking his head in bafflement.

"I thought so," Joe said. "The gang's been transporting diamonds in the tailposts of airplanes." He told Cook about the stones they had found on the landing strip at Marlin Crag.

"And I'll bet this is the tailpost from Chet's fuselage," Joe went on. "Mudd must have realized after the sale that it still had the empty container in it."

"But why did they steal the whole fuselage?"

Cook asked, puzzled. "Why not just the tailpost?"

"They had no time to take it off," Joe reasoned. "So they loaded up the fuselage and were gone in a few minutes."

"A good deduction," Mr. Hardy agreed. "But we still don't know who sent the diamonds and who received them, or why the shipment went to Marlin Crag."

Lieutenant Cook looked thoughtful. "Mr. Hardy, why don't we all get some sleep here before daybreak. Then I suggest you have a talk with the airport personnel, while I see if our dragnet has located the mobile X-ray."

Mr. Hardy and Joe settled down in comfortable chairs and fell into an uneasy sleep. They awakened about eight o'clock, had breakfast at a nearby diner, and then set off to question Steve Holmes, the airport manager.

He insisted he knew nothing about the diamonds.

"Perhaps Bill Zinn can help us," Mr. Hardy said.

"He's away on vacation," Holmes replied.

"Did he leave an address?" Joe asked.

Holmes shook his head.

"What about Dale Nettleton?"

"Sorry, I can't help you there either. Last time I saw Nettleton, he was flying to Morrisville."

"That sounds pretty fishy," Joe murmured.

"We have two suspects who disappear at the same time!"

Just then Holmes's telephone rang. He picked it up, listened a moment, and then handed the phone to Mr. Hardy. "For you," he said.

The Bayport sleuth spoke briefly and hung up. "The police have made a discovery," he said. "We'll have to go." Rapidly he led the way out of the terminal.

"What's up?" Joe queried.

"They found the van."

"Where?"

"In the woods. Lieutenant Cook told me how to get there."

Father and son hastened to the scene. Two police cars were guarding the area.

Parked in a glen and partly concealed by overhanging tree branches stood the large van. The words MOBILE X-RAY stood out boldly on both sides.

The Hardys hastened up to it and around to the rear. Both doors stood open.

The van was empty!

CHAPTER XIX

Needle Man

LIEUTENANT Cook walked up to the Hardys.

"Is this the way you found the van?" Joe asked him.

"Yes. Except that it was locked. Whatever has been in the van was removed before we got here."

Joe pointed to a set of tracks on the floor of the vehicle. "A large box must have been slid out and hidden somewhere, Lieutenant. Frank's probably in it!"

Cook nodded. "I'm having my men scour the woods. But chances are the container has been taken to a building, and not necessarily in this area."

"Well, while you're conducting your search," Mr. Hardy said tersely, "I'll go back to the airport and see what I can find out there. Joe, I suggest you return to the Flickering Torch. It's closed today, but stake it out anyhow. The gang might meet there and perhaps you'll be able to pick up a clue. We'll call you, Lieutenant, if there is any news."

"Good plan," the officer agreed.

"I don't want to waste any time," Mr. Hardy went on. "Could one of your men drop Joe off at the Torch?"

"Sure."

Lieutenant Cook ordered an officer to drive Joe there at once. Minutes later Mr. Hardy set off for the airport in his car. He was just about to leave the parking lot when he heard Chet Morton's jalopy backfire into an open space.

The detective intercepted him. "Chet! What in the world are you doing here?"

"Where's Frank? Did you find him?" Chet asked with a worried look.

"Not yet. How did you know he was missing?"

"Biff called me. And I feel terrible, Mr. Hardy. I've let my buddies down. Frank and Joe were working hard on this case, and what was I doing? Making out like Snoopy and the Red Baron!"

"Don't blame yourself, Chet," Mr. Hardy said. "You couldn't have prevented—"

"But maybe I could have!" Chet said grimly. "Gee, Mr. Hardy, what can I do to help find Frank?"

The detective thought for a moment. "As a matter of fact, there is something you can do. But you'll have to apply all the sleuthing you ever learned from Frank and Joe."

"I'll do it. What is it?"

"Joe went back to the Flickering Torch to stake out the place. It might be a good idea if you'd tail him."

"Me? Tail Joe? What for?"

"He may be in danger. If anything happens to him, you can report to me."

"All right," Chet said.

Mr. Hardy cautioned him to park the car far from the Flickering Torch so that his noisy jalopy would not be a giveaway.

"Don't worry," Chet said, sliding behind the wheel. "I'll hide this in the woods half a mile from the place."

Chet rumbled out of the parking lot. True to his word, he concealed his car in a thicket far from the restaurant, then walked parallel to the road, making sure that nobody saw him.

Several hundred yards from the Flickering Torch Chet parted some bushes and peered at the place, just in time to see Joe slipping around the side of the building. Chet followed, carefully keeping a screen of trees between him and his friend.

Joe reached the window of the manager's office, raised his head slowly, and peered in. Two persons were inside! One was a tall, dark man sitting in a swivel chair. The other was Seymour. The window was slightly ajar and Joe could hear Seymour speaking angrily.

"Bozar, I want to know what's going on!"

Joe thought, "So that's Bozar, the manager of the Flickering Torch!" He strained to hear more of the conversation.

"Sure, Seymour," Bozar said. "What's your complaint?"

"I've been running errands for Mudd—" Seymour began.

"Why not?" Bozar interrupted. "Mudd owns the Flickering Torch. And anyway, he paid you every time, didn't he?"

"The money's fine," Seymour retorted. "But O. K. never tells me what his errands are about. I've never asked any questions, either. But now Frank Hardy's missing. And there seems to be something awfully strange going on around here."

There was silence for a few seconds. Then Bozar said, "So now you're asking questions?"

"You bet your life I am," Seymour said. "And I want some answers."

There was the sound of a scraping chair. Joe saw Bozar stand up. "Seymour, I think you're right. It's time you were let in on the whole deal. But Mudd'll have to do it, he's the boss."

"Where is he?" Seymour demanded.

"Go to the Midatlantic warehouse at 10 Walker Road, near Helen Avenue in Beemerville. You'll find him there. I'll phone ahead so he'll be waiting for you. You have your car here?"

"Yeah. Out in front of the garage."

Joe's mind was in a turmoil. Was Mudd out on

bail? And how could he follow Seymour? He quickly made a decision. Sneaking up to the garage, he saw a red Ford in front of it. There was no other car in sight, so it had to be Seymour's.

Joe quickly opened the door, got in and flattened himself on the floor in the rear and waited tensely.

A minute or so later Seymour slid behind the wheel. He started the engine and headed toward Beemerville.

Watching from hiding, Chet raced back to his jalopy. He started it with the usual bang, then set out in pursuit of the red Ford. After two miles he caught up, but stayed far enough behind to avoid suspicion.

Fifteen minutes later Seymour parked in a deserted neighborhood and got out. Joe peered through the window and saw warehouses on both sides of the street.

Seymour went up to one of them and knocked loudly. The door opened and the youth slipped in. Joe heard a click as the door closed again.

Quickly Joe followed and cautiously tried the knob. It was locked! Stepping back, he looked up at the windows high above. His best chance to get at them was from the roof of a taller building so close that it nearly touched the warehouse.

"There's about ten feet between them," Joe mused. "Maybe I'll be able to see something." He ran to the fire escape of the second structure and climbed to the roof. Hastening across to the parapet, he found himself facing a window six feet below where he was standing. It was blacked out with thick paint!

Disappointed, Joe was about to descend when he spotted a ladder lying on the pebbly roof near a chimney. He carried it to the parapet, lifted it over the edge, and allowed the legs to slide down until they rested on the sill of the warehouse window. The ladder now ran between the two building at an angle.

Beneath Joe was a twenty-five-foot drop to the pavement. He tested the stability of the ladder before gingerly placing his feet on one rung. Letting go of the parapet, he climbed down.

The window was slightly open at the top, but Joe could not see through the crack. Quickly he pulled out his pocketknife and scraped away enough paint for a view inside. Then he put one eye on the glass.

On the warehouse floor sat an enormous boxlike container! Joe could see enough of the interior to make out scientific instruments ranged along one wall. A portable laboratory! At the far end of the warehouse was a delivery van.

Joe's heart beat with excitement as his eye picked out a group to the side of the box. Seymour Schill was flanked by two men in white coats. He looked frightened, but defiant.

"I want to know what's going on here! And no

more of your soft talk! Where is O. K. Mudd?" he demanded.

"He's been arrested. You'll have to be satisfied with us," one of the men replied.

"Who are you?"

"Dr. John Weber. This is my assistant, Dr. Curtice Cain."

Dr. Cain gave a cool nod and disappeared into the lab.

"I never heard of you," Seymour growled.

"Well, we've heard of you, Mr. Schill. You've been our courier, only you didn't know it."

Dr. Weber grinned. "You arranged to get us isotopes in exchange for diamonds."

Seymour looked startled. "So that's what Mudd was up to. Nice little racket!"

"Very nice, indeed," Dr. Weber replied. "And we want it to keep going."

"Too bad you can't," Seymour snorted. "I'm reporting you to the police. This is the end of the line for you!"

"Not for us!" Dr. Weber snarled. "For you!"

He threw himself on Seymour and the pair tumbled to the warehouse floor.

"Curtice, help!" Weber yelled.

Cain came running from the lab bearing a hypodermic needle. He plunged it into Seymour's arm. The guitarist went unconscious.

Working rapidly, Weber and Cain drew a tarpaulin from a compartment of the lab. They spread it on the floor, shifted Seymour onto it, and wrapped him up like a mummy.

Then the two went into the lab, each emerging a moment later with another body swathed in the same way.

"We'll make it to the airport just in time," Weber said as the two men went to get stretchers, one for each of the tarp-shrouded figures.

"They'll be waiting for us," Cain remarked, and opened the back door of the delivery van. He helped Weber to slide the stretchers inside.

The door slammed shut. Cain turned the handle to lock it into place, then he got into the front seat beside Weber, who started the engine.

The hair rose on the nape of Joe's neck. "Frank might be on one of those stretchers!" he thought. "Somehow I'll have to stop that truck!"

Frantically he grabbed the first rung of the ladder and began to ascend. A sound on the other end made him look up. He stared into the menacing face of Bozar!

"See anything that takes your fancy?" the man asked with a smirk and gave the ladder a violent kick. It rose and stood poised for an instant on the window sill, then it fell back, striking heavily against the parapet.

The force of the blow caused Joe to lose his balance. He slipped and plunged toward the pavement twenty-five feet below!

CHAPTER XX

Airport Ambush

JOE uttered a cry and flung out his arms in desperation. The fingers of his right hand closed over the side of the ladder and he clutched it, causing it to turn. Then, with an iron effort, he grasped the ladder with the other hand, and, feet dangling, righted it again.

As he swung his body upward, Bozar shouted, "It's all over, kid. You're going down!" He raised his foot to give the ladder another kick.

But suddenly the man flipped back from the parapet onto the roof. Chet Morton had him in a bear hug!

Joe regained his footing on the ladder in time to see Bozar break away, and a wild slugging match ensued. Bozar went down from a blow to the jaw. He scrambled to his feet, caught Chet with a kick in the stomach, and fled down the fire escape.

Joe climbed to the roof and helped his friend

up. Blood trickled from Chet's nose. He brushed it aside with the back of his hand and grinned. "Your dad told me to shadow you, just in case."

"Great thinking!" Joe said. "Come on. Let's get down. We've got to stop a truck!"

The two rushed to the fire escape, where they spotted Bozar far below running toward the truck. He jumped in beside the driver, then the vehicle roared off.

"He's going to the airport!" Joe panted. "We'll follow!"

Reaching the alley, the boys rushed to Chet's jalopy. Chet started the motor, but it stalled seconds later with a depressing groan.

"That's all we need!" Chet moaned and turned the key again. No action!

"You're out of gas!" Joe exclaimed. "Look!"

Chet threw a desperate glance at the fuel gauge. Joe was right.

Just then two motorcycles whined up the street. Their youthful riders wore leather jackets, helmets, and goggles. Joe jumped out of the car, ran in front of them, and waved his hands. They screeched to a stop a few feet away.

"Fellows, we're out of gas and we've got to get to the airport to stop some crooks from getting away. Can you give us a ride?"

"Why not?" one of the boys said. "Hop on!"

Chet and Joe got on the back seats and the four sped toward Marlin Crag. On the way, the Bayporters gave their rescuers a quick explanation of what the chase was all about.

A short time later Fenton Hardy watched the delivery van drive into the airfield and head for a small plane far out on the runway.

The van stopped and the driver and his two companions leaped out. Hurriedly they opened the doors, and transferred three mummy-like bodies on stretchers to the aircraft. The pilot and another man emerged from the plane and gave them a hand.

Sensing trouble, Mr. Hardy jumped into his car and raced toward the runway. The engine of the plane started with a roar. The backwash of the propeller threw up a cloud of dust. The craft began to move while the detective was still twenty yards away.

Suddenly two motorcycles whizzed past him in a furious staccato of noise and came abreast of the taxiing airplane, one on each side. Two figures jumped off the back seats and grabbed the tail. The plane was so heavily loaded that the pilot had had trouble gathering speed, and the action slowed the craft down.

Quickly Mr. Hardy drove up to the front and cut across the plane's path, compelling it to stop.

Nettleton glared furiously out the window as the two Hardys gathered next to the cockpit door. Zinn, who sat beside him, shook his fist. Behind them appeared the faces of Bozar, Weber, and Cain. All were fuming.

The commotion had alerted the airport police. They rushed up in two patrol cars and surrounded the plane. "Come out with your hands up!" an officer shouted through a bullhorn. Minutes later the five criminals were handcuffed and led to a squad car.

Two officers entered the plane and brought out the three stretchers. Joe and his father quickly ripped the tarps away from the bodies and revealed Frank, Lefty, and Seymour. They were breathing heavily.

"We'll need an ambulance," one of the policemen said. "Jack, go call—"

"Wait," Fenton Hardy interrupted. "This may look worse than it is."

He bent over Frank, who blinked his eyes and sat up. "Wow!" he muttered. "I thought I'd wake up in the briny deep!"

Seymour and Lefty also regained consciousness after two of the policemen had administered first aid.

Mr. Hardly quickly clued in the officer in charge, and told him that the State Police were working on the case.

"Good. We'll take the prisoners right down there," the officer said.

"We'll follow in my car," Mr. Hardy suggested.

Joe and Chet thanked their motorcycle friends, who had thoroughly enjoyed the chase. "It was a pleasure," they assured the boys and rode off with big grins on their faces.

Lieutenant Cook had sandwiches and coffee waiting for everyone at his office, and the Hardys, Chet, Seymour, and Lefty hungrily devoured the food while piecing together the latest events.

A trooper fingerprinted the prisoners, advised them of their rights, and brought them in.

"They wanted to get rid of us," Frank said, pointing to the quintet, "because we knew too much about the airport thefts they had going, especially the uranium isotopes."

Lefty shuddered. "That night in Newark I meant to tell you Zinn was the top guy in the gang, working through the Midatlantic Distribution Corporation. As assistant airport manager, he could keep tabs on what shipments were coming in."

"And he had his pilots fly without vacuum pumps whenever they transported isotopes. That's why Scott and Martin crashed when the weather was bad," Frank deduced. "And he removed the telltale isotopes before the wrecks were investigated."

"When Zinn learned we were searching for information about the crashes," Joe added, "he knew he had to get us out of the way."

"Sure," Chet put in. "He spied on us in

Holmes's office, heard that we were going to Mudd's, and called Mudd to eliminate us."

"Luckily he failed," Frank said. "Even though he tried it three times."

"What do you mean *three* times!" Zinn protested. "Only twice—the business of the crane and the airplane wing, and the junkyard truck that smashed your car."

"Didn't Mudd sabotage the steering mechanism of our car?"

Zinn shook his head. "That must have been strictly coincidental."

"One thing I don't understand," Frank said, looking at Nettleton. "Why did you buzz us when we flew to Marlin Crag the first time? You didn't know us then!"

"Oh, didn't I?" Nettleton sneered. "You think we were stupid? We found out your father was on the case and kept tabs on all of you. When I saw your plane number, I knew what you were up to!"

"But you missed, and you missed again that night at the cliffs when we were looking for the engine," Joe put in. "Also you failed in sabotaging our boat."

"If that big-mouth trucker hadn't let you in on where he dropped the engine, we'd have been all right," Nettleton growled. "You just can't trust people."

"Tell me something," Mr. Hardy said. "How

do Mudd and the Flickering Torch fit into your setup?"

"Figure it out yourself," Nettleton snapped and sullenly looked at his fingernails.

"Maybe Mudd will tell us," Lieutenant Cook suggested, then ordered one of his men to bring in the junk dealer.

"You idiot!" Zinn hissed when he entered. "If you hadn't botched up the job two weeks ago, we wouldn't be in this mess!"

"Oh, shut up!" Mudd muttered. "You had the chance to shoot those nosy brats and what did *you* do? Nothing!"

Curtice Cain, meanwhile, was arguing with Weber. "I told you we should never have gotten involved with these people! Everything went well as long as they didn't know who we were!"

"Wait a minute," Mr. Hardy said. "Who didn't know who you were?"

"These—these stupid, ignorant, amateur smugglers!" Cain fumed, pointing at Zinn and his buddies.

Now a strange story unfolded. Weber and Cain had developed a new, inexpensive process of making industrial diamonds from coal through the use of uranium isotopes. By way of the criminal underground grapevine they had learned of the freight thieves and had begun buying the illicit isotopes from them without ever meeting any of the gang in person. In their mobile lab Weber and Cain changed the structure of the coal by means of the isotopes. Then they turned the product over to an unethical manufacturer in the New York area who completed the process.

The isotopes were deposited in specially fitted lead containers in the amplifiers at the Flickering Torch and Pete Guilfoyle's barn. Weber and Cain would then pick them up at odd hours and leave the payment.

"Joe, when we went to the Flickering Torch the first time, we saw Nettleton fooling around with the amp!" Frank said. "He either made a delivery or picked up the payment!"

"No kidding!" Nettleton said sarcastically. "And if you're real smart, you'll tell me which one it was!"

"Probably both," said Joe. "And how do you like this: Last Wednesday night you went to Guilfoyle's barn in the rain, took a container with diamonds from the amp, deposited isotopes, and left. Then Weber and Cain picked up the loot when the weather had cleared."

Nettleton glared at Weber. "That's when you got us in trouble. Mudd told you no more rocks! I took the stuff to Morrisville and my contact refused to accept them!"

"So you brought them back and lost a couple in a bum landing," Joe completed the thought.

Nettleton shrugged.

"How come you and Zinn let me check out

your plane that day?" Frank asked. "You did transport diamonds in the tailpost!"

Nettleton grinned. "By the time you were through with my suitcase, Zinn had already removed the container."

"Another thing I don't understand," Frank went on, "is why you hid the diamonds in the tailpost, but the isotopes in the vacuum pump housing?"

"We couldn't take the isotopes out of the lead container, and it didn't fit in the tailpost. We therefore had to find another good hiding spot, and the vacuum pump seemed the best."

"Who's Nick?" Joe inquired, changing the subject.

Mudd pointed his thumb at Bozar. "It's his nickname."

"You gotta tell 'em everything?" Bozar grumbled. "You a big believer in confessions or what?"

"Your voice seems familiar," Mr. Hardy put in. "You called me when you caught Lefty and told me to lay off, didn't you?"

Bozar did not answer.

Frank turned to Lefty. "It was Zinn's heavies who waylaid you in Newark. How did you ever wind up with Weber?"

"I was taken to the Midatlantic warehouse in Beemerville. They kept me there tied up until the van came in," Lefty replied. "Then this guy" —he pointed to Weber—"gave me a shot in the arm and I don't remember anything from that moment on."

"Which brings us to the last link in the case," Lieutenant Cook said, looking from Zinn to Weber. "How did you two ever get together?"

"It was a mistake," Weber said resignedly. "We knew that the Hardys were working on the freight case, and should have stayed as far away from the gang as possible. But yesterday a plane circled over the van and we felt sure they were on to us, too. The first thing we had to do was hide the lab, so I got in touch with Zinn and asked him for shelter. He told us to put the portable lab in the warehouse. Then we drove the empty van back into the woods to mislead the Hardys."

"Which was another mistake," Zinn grumbled.

"Where did you plan to go today?" Cook continued his questioning.

"When we found out this morning that Mudd had been arrested, we figured the jig was up. We called Zinn, who said they were leaving for Canada and offered to take us along. We decided to give up the lab, despite the large investment and save our lives. Lefty, Frank Hardy, and Schill knew too much and had to be eliminated. Rather than poisoning them in the warehouse and leaving them as evidence, we decided to take them on the plane and drop them into the ocean."

"Nice thought," Frank muttered. "You're awfully kind."

"I have another question," Joe spoke up. "Someone seemed to be spying on me and the boys last Wednesday night at Pete Guilfoyle's barn. Who was it?"

"Curtice kept the place under surveillance since we had a pickup at night. We usually did that, just a routine precaution."

Joe nodded. "I also found a guitar pick outside the barn."

"No wonder, with all those musicians around," Nettleton said.

"Coming back to the beginning of the whole thing," Frank said to Zinn, "did your pilots know they were transporting contraband?"

"No. Martin Weiss and Jack Scott became suspicious but crashed before they found out anything definite."

"How come the FAA didn't find the isotopes?"

"We got there ahead of them," Zinn replied.

The telephone rang and Lieutenant Cook answered. When he had finished, he said, "That was the Morrisville police. They have closed down the Midatlantic operation and arrested all suspects, including a pilot. Late last night Scotland Yard made their move in London and got the exporters of the isotopes, who in turn revealed their contacts in New York. The New York police are rounding up everyone on that end. Which just about solves our case."

"As far as the isotopes are concerned," Frank

agreed. "But what about the other freight heists?"

"The cargo was either flown to Morrisville, New Jersey, or trucked to various locations in New York State. The Morrisville and New York police have all the information on that. And, what's more, they know the names of everyone concerned with the distribution. It'll take a few days to round up all the people connected, but thanks to Mr. Hardy we know exactly whom to look for."

Mr. Hardy grinned. "It was a hard case to crack, but as Frank once said, 'the harder the better!'"

The young sleuths relaxed momentarily in the glow of success. But another knotty mystery, to be known as *The Melted Coins,* was to challenge the Hardys in the near future.